John Go

Crocky and the Easter Bunny

Bumblebee
Books

A CIP catalogue record for this title is
available from the British Library.

ISBN: 978-1-83934-806-8

Bumblebee Books is an imprint of
Olympia Publishers.

First Published in 2022

Bumblebee Books
Tallis House
2 Tallis Street
London
EC4Y 0AB
Printed in Great Britain

Dedication

I dedicate this book to my parents, my wife, Jane, and our children, Callum, Harry, and Sophie.

Chapter One

Easter Escape

"Come back here!" shouted a sprinting Easter Bunny.

Similar cries were exploding from a very angry crowd of assorted animals, who were racing with her. They were chasing a panic-stricken, slightly-built, two-feet-long crocodile.

Crocky was what his friends called him. Many in the chasing pack were calling him a thief and much worse. He had just come hurtling out of Easter Bunny Meadow, which was a secret underground complex in beautiful rural Devon. He was heading towards the nearby River Otter at top speed.

It was an amazing spectacle for a quiet Palm Sunday morning – or for any time for that matter. Crocky was running as fast as he could on his hind legs. He was covered in feathers. Whilst they were mainly from chickens, the effects of Crocky dashing across the uneven and muddy ground caused a blizzard of plumage to fly out behind him and over the following animals. As he lost more feathers, it soon became apparent that his costume was actually constructed out of a variety of other avian sources too. These included duck, goose, pheasant and partridge.

The only feather-free parts of Crocky were his mouth and snout. These were also disguised but by a curved piece of toughened plastic. This had once been positioned to look like a bright orange beak. Crocky's rapid progress away from his pursuers, though, had caused this facial adornment to become partly detached. This left it flapping and slapping over Crocky's nose like a loose letterbox in a gale. However, Crocky was panicking too much to notice any discomfort or lack of sartorial elegance.

Despite his desperate efforts to escape, the animals were gaining on Crocky constantly. Those closest to him were furiously trying their utmost to get within range to peck, grab, strike or do a whole number of other unpleasant things to the fleeing crocodile. The front of this mob had nearly caught up with Crocky as he reached the riverbank. Without pausing for thought, Crocky flung himself as far as he could over the water and away from the chasing pack. For a split second, he appeared to hover above the river as if suspended in mid-air.

SPLASH!

Crocky's brief experience of gravity-defying came to a crashing end with an enormous, watery belly-flop.

The creatures left on dry land skidded to a halt. There were a number of audible, sharp intakes of breath rippling through the crowd. No one had really expected Crocky to do that. They shuffled towards the water's edge and stopped as closely as they could without falling in. Their shock did not last long. Within half a minute or so, many of the animals started clucking and shouting in fury once more. Some of the birds were so angry they were nearly spitting actual feathers.

Everyone looked intently into the watery abyss, trying to find Crocky.

As hard as they tried, the result was:

Nothing.

They continued to stare into and along the river:

Nothing.

They peered up and down the riverbanks:

Nothing.

As the minutes passed:

Nothing.

The Easter Bunny made her way slowly to the front of the group, stopping very carefully about a foot away from taking a dip herself. The river may have looked really pretty in the spring morning sunshine, but its waters were still extremely cold. The Easter Bunny certainly did not fancy a swim in it. She raised a front paw and cleared her throat. Instantly, everyone fell silent.

"Dear friends. He's gone. Unfortunately, he seems to have eaten all of our Easter eggs."

Gasps of shock and horror rippled through the assembled crowd. Tears began welling up in many eyes. Sensing the despair, the Easter Bunny hurriedly tried to rally everyone.

"Dear Friends. Easter is only a week away. We mustn't let this one naughty crocodile ruin it for all the children. We won't let him!"

Her eyes narrowed and she looked at the animals in front of her with firm determination.

"We won't let him ruin it for anyone!" shouted the Easter Bunny.

Cheers started to ring out.

She continued, "Please wipe your eyes, blow your beaks, bills and noses. Work with me to save Easter. Together, we will save Easter!"

As the Easter Bunny proclaimed this final sentence, she raised her paw even higher into the air, only now pointing her forefinger to the heavens. The whole crowd was cheering. As they reached a crescendo of noise, they broke out into spontaneous chants of, "We'll save Easter, We'll save Easter!"

"And what is more," added the Easter Bunny, using all the strength in her voice to be heard, "I've just come off the emergency helpline to my good friend in the North. He is sending help – lots of it!"

The Easter Bunny and Father Christmas are really good friends. They are very much in the same line of business – to bring joy and happiness to children all over the world. Good friends will always help each other in a time of crisis; and this really was a crisis. All of the Easter eggs for England had to be replaced in less than a week. That was many millions of Easter eggs.

Santa and the Easter Bunny had set up an emergency phone line between them many years ago. It was only to be called in truly exceptional times. The line was linked to no one else. It had never been used before. In fact when Santa's emergency phone rang that Palm Sunday, he was so surprised he nearly jumped out of his big red coat! He offered and sent practical help immediately to Easter Bunny Meadow.

Above the heads of all those assembled on that riverbank, there was a rumble, then a whoosh. Suddenly, the sky was filled with what appeared to be countless green creatures parachuting down to the meadow.

One chicken screamed, "Help! It's the crocodile's friends!"

Nearly the whole crowd looked up in panic; but one cool head prevailed. An older chicken, stick under her right wing, waddled duck-like, slowly but purposefully, to the front of the fearful masses. She had a beautiful, golden embroidered, royal blue dress. She wore sparkling glasses, which were perched half-way down her brilliantly shiny orange beak. Behind those spectacles were the most alive and kind eyes. She tapped her stick loudly on the ground.

This was Prudence. She was President of Easter Bunny Meadow's Federation of Easter and Spring Time Unions and Societies (EASTUS). She looked after the interests of all the animals working and living there. When she spoke, everybody listened. She spoke in a clear, authoritative and strong voice.

"Come now. Look to the North... In the sky there... Do crocodiles come from a reindeer-driven sleigh?" pointed out Prudence reassuringly.

The Easter Bunny smiled to herself. Prudence was her best friend and confidante at Easter Bunny Meadow. The Easter Bunny and Prudence ran this complex together. Their philosophy was for everyone to work together with love and respect.

"Thank you, Prudence," laughed the Easter Bunny, addressing the crowd again. "They are not naughty crocodiles. They may like wearing a lot of green; they can sometimes be a bit mischievous; but they are elves. I called Santa. He is my friend in the North. I told him about our problems. He has sent us his Christmas Chocolate Makers to help get our Easter eggs back on track. Please make them welcome and we will rescue this situation together."

Everyone looked up. They could now make out a large number of elves floating down. High up in the sky, between fluffy white, cotton wool clouds, they could see the reindeer-driven sleigh, which had delivered them. As the sleigh turned for its trip back to the North Pole, they could see a person in a red cloak in the driver's seat giving them a cheery wave.

Huge cheers rang out from the ground for Santa and the elves. All the animals flocked to welcome their new friends as they landed. Easter was going to be saved. Just as the Easter Bunny had promised.

The Easter Bunny looked over at the chicken who had raised the false alarm. She looked embarrassed and nervous. The Easter Bunny placed a loving paw on her shoulder.

"You did well there, Chomper. You were the first person to spot our new arrivals. You didn't know they were our friends. How could you? Only Prudence and I knew the elves were coming; and from that high in the sky, they did look very green!"

Chomper flashed a big and relieved grin to the Easter Bunny.

"Thank you," responded Chomper, in a half-whisper.

Chapter Two

As Rare as Hens' Teeth

Charlie "Chomper" Chicken was a special member of the workforce at Easter Bunny Meadow. She was caring, hard-working, keen to learn, and the only chicken there who had teeth. Yes, she hatched with teeth; that is how she gained her nickname of Chomper. Out of the many thousands of chickens that had ever been in Easter Bunny Meadow, she was the only one with teeth. Chomper used to be self-conscious about this. This feeling was made worse because some other animals could be unkind when they looked at Chomper or talked about her. All that changed, though, on one eventful day.

Two summers before Crocky was chased out of Easter Bunny Meadow, a lost and drunken fox had stumbled his way there. Grandeur Fox was his name.

Grandeur had spent a most enjoyable afternoon with the Badger family sampling a glass, or seven, of Bertie Badger's finest, home-made, honeydew wine.

As the afternoon had well and truly turned into evening, Grandeur realised that he should have been home a couple of hours earlier. His family had only asked him to do one thing for them that day, which was to come home with dinner for them. Of course, he had completely forgotten about this.

Oh bother, he thought to himself.

He bid his farewells to the Badgers hurriedly, before leaving their home and setting off down their quiet country lane to start his journey home. A mixture of the cool evening air and Grandeur's quite rapid change from a long period of sitting down drinking to walking along a rutted track, suddenly made him realise that he was quite tipsy. It also set off uncontrollable and very loud hiccups.

"I am so in trouble... *hiccup!* Oh and now... *hiccup...* I have... *hiccup...* the hiccups... *hiccup!* I hate the hiccups... *hiccup, hiccup!*" muttered the fed-up fox to himself.

His hiccups became louder and his temper became shorter. He became so consumed with drunken anger that he stopped paying proper attention to where he was walking. He became hopelessly lost. When he realised this, he started to panic. Panic and intoxication are not a good mix. He tripped and rolled into a pile of mud.

SPLAT!

By the time he had staggered to his feet again, he was dizzy, dirty and dishevelled: no more grandeur for Grandeur! But at least the fright had cured his hiccups!

Wholly unknown to Grandeur, he had stumbled just outside the entrance to Easter Bunny Meadow. Grandeur looked around him. He saw the River Otter nearby with three chickens standing on its bank. They had come from Easter

Bunny Meadow after a hard day's work. They were trying to spot any of the Trout family that lived along that stretch of water.

Aha! thought Grandeur to himself. *Things are looking up. There's my dinner. There's my escape from a massive telling off when I get home.*

Half-staggering, the fox tried his inebriated best to creep up behind the chickens. Just as he made his ungainly move, the Trout children – two-year-old twins Tina and Tiny – came out from under some hanging branches that kissed the river's surface. They swam over to say hello to the chickens. The chickens were overjoyed and enchanted to see the youngsters. They were waving their wings at the young fish, clucking and giggling all over them. In their happiness, they were oblivious to the impending danger.

"Just a couple of yards more," Grandeur told himself as he edged closer to the chickens. The fox licked his lips thinking of a large chicken feast and in drunken pride of how clever he was.

He thought to himself, *Seven glasses of honeydew wine and I can still grab a large dinner. What a fox you are, Grandeur!*

As Grandeur moved for what he hoped was the dinner strike, he had failed to spot what was happening behind him. At that moment, Chomper had come out of Easter Bunny Meadow and she was approaching the riverbank for some post-work relaxation.

Chomper was, and still is, tough, fearless and loyal to her friends and colleagues. These traits have caused her parents no end of worries over her young life, but that was Chomper.

All chickens are taught from a very young age about the dangers of wild foxes. Chomper had never seen a real-life wild fox before. Her view of wild foxes, though, was quite simple.

She would tell anyone who asked her, "No stuck-up wild fox is going to get the better of me. They may have smart coats but pretty fur does not make them any better than chickens! If I ever come across any wild fox causing problems to any chicken, I will certainly teach them a lesson or two!"

When Chomper saw Grandeur ahead of her, without even a nanosecond of consideration for her own safety, she thought, *A wild fox. I'll show him!*

If truth be told, Chomper had not considered the real danger that her friends and she were in. She just saw a fox and decided to sort him out.

Grandeur was just a couple of feet away from dinner when Chomper flew at him like a feathered guided missile.

A sober fox would have noticed a not-so-aerodynamic chicken charging towards him. However, an ale-induced hunger and a fuzzy brain had completely focussed Grandeur's mind on dinner to the exclusion of everything else.

CHOMP!

Chomper sank her not inconsiderable teeth into the first part of the fox that she reached: his long bushy tail.

"*OWWWW!*" screamed Grandeur.

He turned his head sharply. In his alcohol-addled shock, all he could make out behind him was a blur of orange, brown and white. Nevertheless, he could clearly feel that this blur had sunk a set of really sharp and strong teeth into his tail. His mind went into rapid overdrive. He knew that no wild Devonian creature would try to eat a strong fox like him. He decided that he must have been bitten by a young escaped lion. It then dawned upon him that wherever there was a young lion, there could very well be mummy and daddy lions nearby too. There was no way he was going to wait for them to turn up!

In terror, Grandeur leapt into the river. As he jumped, he felt a piece of his tail tear off. He swam and swam until his paws could swim no more. He never returned.

The three chickens, whose lives Chomper had just saved, turned around to view the source of this cacophony. The Trout children whooshed under a large rock and waited for their parents to take them to home. Their parents were slightly delayed coming to their children because they were nearly flattened by a panicking fox jumping into and flailing around in the river.

Those three chickens quickly worked out what had happened, particularly when they saw Chomper standing there with a large piece of fox tail in her beak.

The Easter Bunny came hopping over at top speed. She was followed by a large number of her colleagues. Whilst the three chickens explained excitedly what had happened, Chomper just stood quietly as if starting to contemplate the enormity of what she had done.

"Well, Charlie, your bravery is amazing. You are a hero!" exclaimed the Easter Bunny. She continued with a chuckle, "By the way, you don't have to eat that tail. Humans might eat oxtails in soup, but I've never heard of fox-tail soup!"

That comment brought Chomper out of her daze. She looked down her beak at the part of Grandeur's tail that was still in her mouth, and decided it tasted disgustingly awful.

"*Yeuch!*" shrieked Chomper, spitting it out into the floor. "I'll leave it for the crows."

"*Caw.* Thank you. I'll come back for it shortly. It'll make a good supper," shouted Colin Crow, who was flying back to his nest high-up in the willow trees that lined the riverbank.

The Easter Bunny put a proud and kindly paw around Chomper. Then a number of her friends and colleagues came and raised Chomper up high on their shoulders, cheering and celebrating her achievement. Her parents and wider family joined the throng and beamed with pride. That night, everyone at Easter Bunny Meadow held an impromptu party for Chomper as guest of honour.

That day did two things. Firstly, Chomper decided she liked that nickname and asked everyone to use it. Secondly, no one ever saw anything strange or funny about a chicken having teeth again. Everyone is unique and difference is something to celebrate.

Grandeur Fox found a route out of the river and made his sodden way home. The one thing that a mixture of Chomper's actions and the freezing river had done was make him feel sobered up rather quickly. Unfortunately for him, his hopes of providing his family with a large, or any, dinner were well and truly lost. When he arrived home and tried to explain himself, his very hungry family were not impressed; not impressed at all.

There's an old human expression that you are in the doghouse when you really upset someone close to you. When you are a wild dog and you really upset your nearest and dearest, you get thrown out of the doghouse!

This is particularly true when you return home very late; your breath smells of stale honeydew wine; you look a complete mess with a chunk missing from your tail, as if you had been involved in a drunken fight; and you have completely failed to come back home with dinner, which was the only thing that you had been asked to do. Then you add to your family's upset by providing them with an explanation of your state and behaviour that involved you being attacked by a lion in the middle of the English countryside. Unsurprisingly, in their eyes, this story lacked a bit of credibility!

The result of all of this was that Grandeur's family threw him out of their doghouse very quickly. He left with what remained of his tail between his legs. Grandeur went to his usual spot, where he always sought refuge or contemplation time when he was in trouble. It was under a hedge just in sight of his home. He settled down feeling very sorry for himself. His mood soon became much worse as within a few minutes, a thunderstorm arrived and tipped huge amounts of extremely heavy rain over him.

"Nice," he muttered sarcastically up to an owl, who was sheltering himself snuggly in a comfortable, dry and warm hole in a nearby tree. The owl winked back at him.

Grandeur sighed as the rain streamed down his face. He called up to the owl, "For once I told the truth when I messed up. I REALLY was attacked by a lion. I'm scarred for life. I'm starving hungry! And this is what happens! *Hmph!*"

The owl just stared at him and started to hoot with laughter.

Chapter Three

Merry Easter

Easter in England that year may have been saved, but some things turned out a little differently. Whilst Easter chocolate is famed for its eggs and animal shapes, like bunnies, lambs and chicks, Santa's chocolate is created in quite different styles.

The elves had been drafted in with no notice. They were still recovering from their intensely busy Christmas schedule. They arrived at Easter Bunny Meadow still tired and never having paid any attention to the look and feel of Easter chocolate. As soon as they arrived and had been welcomed, to their surprise they were transported far away from Easter Bunny Meadow. The reason for this was that the chocolate was not made in the Devon complex at all.

However, elves are extremely proud creatures. They will never admit tiredness, shock or lack of knowledge about anything. They also believe that they are the best present and chocolate makers in the world. They will not accept any suggestion or insinuation otherwise. This meant that they declined any help from the Easter Bunny or any of her colleagues. They even refused to let any of the Easter Bunny's quality control staff check what they were doing.

Erica, the Chief Chocolate-Making Elf, put their opinion

very simply, "Do you think we produce substandard chocolate for Santa at Christmas? Of course not; so, we won't produce substandard chocolate for the Easter Bunny at Easter either. Please leave us alone to get on with our jobs."

The elves knew that time was very short. They decided to focus their initial work on making all of the chocolate. Once they had done that, they would shift their labour to sending the finished products to Easter Bunny Meadow. This meant that the staff at Easter Bunny Meadow had no idea of any potential difficulties until a Bunny Burrow goods train arrived in Devon on Good Friday. There was great joy and excitement as the Easter Bunny Meadow's workers began to unload the first consignment of chocolate from the elves. Those emotions changed very quickly. They moved to surprise, then to shock and culminated in complete panic. A staff delegation was hurriedly assembled. They rushed off to see Prudence in her office. When they arrived there, they found Prudence sharing a pot of tea with the Easter Bunny.

Prudence and the Easter Bunny tried to calm their colleagues without success. They were so upset, talking over each other, that Prudence and the Easter Bunny could not understand a word they were saying.

Prudence and the Easter Bunny stood up from their chairs quickly and said in unison, "Please show us what's wrong."

They followed the concerned group back to the train. When they saw what had caused such consternation, they looked at each other and started to laugh. Their staff looked confused by their reaction. Some started to wonder if the shock had made them become really poorly.

The Easter Bunny looked at the worried faces around her and commented, "It appears that when the children of England wake up on this Easter Sunday, they will discover a few exciting new experiences."

What the Easter Bunny meant was that the elves had made delicious but unusual chocolate treats for Easter. Many an English Easter Egg Hunt that year would reveal a mixture of Easter chocolate canes, bauble shaped 'eggs', Easter Bunnies with bright red noses, Easter Chicks with carrot-shaped orange beaks and striking red chests, and other Easter Bunnies and Easter Chicks adorned with ears that looked more like antlers!

The Easter Bunny carried on, "Friends, we all know that children love Easter chocolate. It's now Good Friday. Our choices are stark. We could cancel all deliveries for England this Easter..."

She paused for effect and looked around the group as murmurs of "No" and "We can't do that" went around.

"Or we deliver this special, one-off, Easter chocolate for the children of England!" she exclaimed with rousing force.

This had the desired effect with nearly all of the assembled workforce cheering and shouting in agreement.

The Easter Bunny then proclaimed, "We won't let the children of England be punished because of one crocodile. Who really cares if this year's chocolate looks a bit different? It's still special chocolate for all the children. It's still really yummy chocolate. I believe many children will love these new shapes. We will keep calm and carry on. We will get this new chocolate ready and I will deliver it all as planned!"

Prudence nodded in agreement.

The workforce cheered again and they started unloading the train, both happy and re-assured.

However, there was one chicken, Chomper, who was there and who still looked worried. She walked over to the Easter Bunny and Prudence.

"But what if the children notice and don't like these new shapes. Won't we be spoiling everything for them? If we spoil things for them this year, don't we risk them remembering their disappointment every Easter and hurting them for years?" asked Chomper earnestly, with rapid verbal delivery.

Prudence and the Easter Bunny smiled at Chomper.

Prudence spoke soothingly but deliberately, "Don't you agree that it's better for the children to get their chocolate treats rather than nothing this year: even if they are a bit... well, different."

Prudence ended her sentence with a friendly chuckle. She knew how to help the mood of any of her colleagues. Chomper relaxed and laughed with her.

"After all, the alternative really is that the children of England would get nothing. Children would get chocolate everywhere else in the world, including every other country in the United Kingdom, except for England. That would be really upsetting and unfair to so many. We also know what some humans can be like. They would probably think that some other country had sabotaged their Easter causing no end of serious problems. We can't allow that, can we?" added Prudence.

Chomper considered this. She knew what some humans could be like.

She shook her head and said, "No, we can't."

Chomper then went back to work, joining her colleagues to ensure that these unusual Easter chocolates would be ready for the Easter Bunny to deliver in less than a couple of days.

What Chomper and her colleagues did not know was that the Easter Bunny and Prudence did have some concerns about what the elves were going to do. However, they knew that Crocky had left them in such a precarious position there was nothing they could do about it other than hope for the best.

Their worries began on the day after Palm Sunday. A very keen elf, called Eldon, had asked if he could show the Easter Bunny a new device that he had made. The Easter Bunny and Prudence went down to the Easter Bunny's Chocolate Development Department to meet him. Very proudly, he unveiled a contraption, which he had concealed against business espionage in a tatty and battered old cardboard box. The Easter Bunny noticed that this container had originally housed bathroom-cleaning products.

With a huge grin, Eldon leant into the box and revealed his Easter Chocolate Medal Dispenser. He put it on a small table to the side of him. This device was about a foot high and most of it was constructed out of metal. It was sturdy and very well-made. It was built to look like an Easter Bunny. This bunny was dressed in a luminous, lime-green cloak adorned with fluorescent, neon-yellow lining. This bunny's fur was a strikingly vivid orange colour, except for its brilliantly white, fluffy tail. The colours were so garishly bright that the Easter Bunny and Prudence wished they had brought their sunglasses.

Eldon demonstrated how the machine worked with obvious joy. It had a remarkably simple operating mechanism. The rabbit's ears started off pointing straight upwards. The elf went to the front of the device, grabbed the ears and pulled them down until they lay at right angles to the top of the bunny's forehead like the peak of a cap. As the ears moved, the bunny opened its mouth, declaring in a loud and booming voice:

"Ho, ho, ho, Merry Easter!"

As it blasted out that message, the rabbit stuck out its tail and a chocolate medal, which looked rather like a chocolate coin, dropped out from under it and onto the table. The medal was wrapped in gold-coloured foil with a drawing of an Easter Bunny upon it.

"There you have it," stated Eldon triumphantly as the medal plopped out. "The coney has produced its chocolate coin, er... I mean medal."

Eldon stood by his work with in a triumphant pose.

The Easter Bunny and Prudence stared back with blank expressions. It was not often they were both lost for words, but this elf had achieved it in quite a short space of time. Prudence noticed this highly unusual occurrence and started to giggle. Something else then came to mind and she started to laugh uncontrollably.

The Easter Bunny and Eldon looked at Prudence, puzzled. Prudence leant over to the Easter Bunny and whispered something in her ear. The Easter Bunny let out a snort and started roaring with laughter too. This only served to confuse the poor elf even more.

The Easter Bunny managed to control her mirth just long enough to give the perplexed elf a thumbs up sign. She spluttered out to him that he had created the funniest Easter chocolate device that she had ever seen.

After a brief pause, she then said, "However, I'm not sure that all parents and guardians would necessarily approve of a laughing bunny feeding their children rabbit droppings from their botties!"

That was the cue for both the Easter Bunny and Prudence to double up with even more laughter before they both staggered up to Eldon, shook his hand, bid him goodbye and wished him well with his next design.

Just before the still bemused elf left the Development Department, the Easter Bunny told him, "Please keep up the good work. We all need some laughter in our lives. I will ensure that I'll give you a special mention to Santa when we next speak."

True to her word she did, which made both Eldon and Father Christmas very happy.

Chapter Four

Crocky, Mermaids and a Mermicorn

Crocky's real name was a bit of a mystery. If anyone asked him for his forename, he'd say, "Crocodile". If they asked him for his surname, he'd say, "Crocodile". If they queried this and asked him why he had the same forename and surname, he'd reply, "If it's good enough for New York, it's good enough for me – *SNAP!*"

So either his real name was Crocodile Crocodile, or he had a name that he did not want to tell anyone. No one except Crocky knew the real answer. In any event, he liked to be called Crocky by those who knew him, so everybody left it at that.

Crocky was not your average crocodile. He was only two feet long from the tip of his tail to the end of his nose. He had learnt to stand up on his hind legs, which gave him a standing height of about twenty inches. He had an insatiable appetite for human food. He did not care what it was, who made it, how it was made or grown, or whose food it was. If it was human food, he would just eat it – very quickly and noisily.

Fate made Crocky who he was. It started before Crocky was born. It was even before his daddy and mummy met.

Many years ago, when Crocky's daddy was a young, single,

adult crocodile, he decided to go travelling around the world alone. He ended up in the eastern Mediterranean Sea having a lovely relaxing time, floating along the surface of the warm, calm water. He was just minding his own business, marvelling at the glorious weather and natural beauty.

Almost immediately below him, a mermaid princess was on an official royal visit to open a new fish pre-school on the sea bed. Crocky's daddy had no idea about it.

His daddy heard the sound of a misfiring boat engine in the distance. He raised a lazy eyebrow and noticed a battered, old, smoke-spewing vessel coming towards him. As the boat passed him at very close quarters, he saw its human crew throwing their rubbish overboard. They were oblivious about anything or anyone around them, and they did not care.

Crocky's daddy managed to avoid being struck by this refuse, but not by much. He watched in disgust as the boat spluttered off towards the coast. The mermaid princess was not so lucky. The rubbish plunged to the bottom of the sea landing right on top of the unsuspecting royal. She was flattened by it and knocked unconscious. It was a horrible mixture of food waste, assorted plastics, metals and old rope. Luckily, it just missed the young pre-school fish students, their teachers and everyone else, but they were so shocked and terrified by what had happened out of the blue that no one felt safe enough to go to the aid of the stricken mermaid princess.

That part of the Mediterranean Sea was so clear that

Crocky's daddy could see right to the seabed. He saw the mermaid princess a split second before the waste struck and buried her. His fury at this sea fly-tipping changed immediately into huge concern for the prone princess. He never liked seeing anyone hurt or in trouble, so as soon he saw the princess's situation, he shot down to her. Using a mixture of his teeth and the strength of a crocodile roll, he managed to untangle her. Then, ever-so-gently, like a mummy crocodile with her baby, he picked up the princess in his extremely strong mouth and most carefully brought her to the water's surface. There he stroked her lovingly with his tongue and slowly woke her up.

When the Princess regained consciousness, the first thing that she saw that she was in the mouth of a very large crocodile. Unsurprisingly, she was petrified. Crocky's daddy had expected that reaction. He spoke to the princess very kindly, respectfully and gently. He quickly re-assured her that he meant her no harm and he explained to her what had happened.

The princess soon understood everything and that she was safe. She had never met such a kind and caring crocodile. She was extremely grateful to him and offered to reward him. Being a shy and modest animal, Crocky's daddy politely declined and said that saving the mermaid princess was reward in itself. He was even too shy and modest to tell her his name.

This endeared Crocky's daddy to the princess even more. She respected his decision but she still wanted to thank him properly. She was very shaken by her experience and she was livid about human rubbish being thrown into the sea. This was something that she knew happened too often all over the world. Without really thinking through the meaning of what she was about to do, she suddenly jumped back from Crocky's daddy, raised her right hand to the sky and cast this magic spell.

"My dear crocodile friend, I make this permanent spell to honour your actions and to teach all humanity a lesson for their wanton disrespect of the waters of the Earth," she bellowed into the air.

The princess continued, "This spell will give all of your children unique protections from humanity and, just as humans plunder, your children will plunder from them until all humans change their ways."

A thunderbolt flashed across the clear blue sky and the mermaid princess disappeared.

Crocky's daddy remained in his position in the sea for a few minutes motionless and stunned; not quite believing what had just happened. The main thing that was going through his mind was how could a magical and powerful mermaid princess pass such a spell without checking his family situation! At the time, he was both single and did not have any children. He did not even have any potential love interest remotely in mind. Then his stomach rumbled and that brought him out of his semi-dazed state. He shrugged his shoulders and swam away looking for some food.

Crocky's daddy had vaguely heard about mermaid magic, but he had never seen any such magic working before. He had no idea about how serious any effects of mermaid magic might be or even if they worked. He also wondered how spells that would only begin to take effect at some unknown time in the future could possibly be activated if there were no mermaids around to start them up! After not too long, his daddy decided that the whole thing was a bit too difficult to understand so he tried to put it to the back of his mind.

In fact, the princess's spell was an extremely serious and powerful thing. It would most definitely work and it did. In fact, when mermaids pass spells that require things to be done in the future, they have found a way to get around the issue that it is not always possible or practical for them to drop everything to make sure they are carried out. Their ingenious solution involved their mermicorn spirit friends.

Mermicorn spirits live in the magic spirit world. As their name says, they are mermicorns, who are also spirits. However, they insist on being called mermicorns. The only time it is acceptable in polite mermicorn spirit society to mention that they are spirits is when giving the official title of their king or queen, which is the King or Queen of the Mermicorn Spirits – currently they have a king. The only reason why their royalty refer to themselves as spirits is because the official title of the king or queen of their non-spirit mermicorn cousins on Earth is the King or Queen of the Mermicorns. Because their Earth-dwelling relatives chose their regal title first, and it would be just too confusing to give them the same official monarchical names, the mermicorn spirit royalty had to be referred to in a slightly different way.

It is never a good idea to offend any magical mermicorns. They always have a host of unpleasant spells that they could cast if they think anyone has been deliberately nasty to them. Therefore, this book will refer to them as mermicorns from now on.

Mermicorns are generally kind and helpful. They are able to keep watch over things on Earth and turn up in an instant if required. They are the perfect beings to help with mermaid spells.

The mermicorns agreed that when any mermaids cast spells, the King of the Mermicorn Spirits would be told automatically. As this was likely to involve rather a lot of spells, the king assembled a team of mermicorns to receive the notifications on his behalf. That team would allocate the spells to mermicorns by Royal Proclamation. Only mermicorns, who had graduated from the Mermicorn Magic College, could be chosen for this role.

Once mermicorns have been allocated spells, they will carry them out, but they have to follow the seven ancient Mermaid and Mermicorn Royal Rules.

Those rules are:

1. Mermicorns must carry out any mermaid spells

allocated to them by Royal Proclamation,

2. Mermicorns must carry out those spells in accordance with how they were originally cast, subject to the following rules,

3. Royal Mermaids may change or cancel any spells cast by non-Royal Mermaids, unless it is a permanent spell,

4. The Mermaid Monarch may also change or cancel any spells cast by Royal Mermaids, including himself of herself, unless it is a permanent spell,

5. Permanent spells cannot be changed or cancelled, and mermicorns must not allow any mermaid of any rank or status do so,

6. Mermicorns are not allowed to travel into the future, and

7. Mermicorns may travel into the past, but when in the past:

(a) Mermicorns must remain invisible,

(b) Mermicorns must not communicate with any creatures or beings, and

(c) Mermicorns must not take part in, assist, change or stop the behaviours or decisions of any creatures or beings.

Over the next few hours after casting her spell, the mermaid princess reflected upon what she had done and those centuries-old Mermaid and Mermicorn Royal Rules. She began to get very worried. The Princess had dreadful thoughts of Crocky's daddy having lots of children. She worried about those children growing to be huge, scary, greedy and impervious to humans. She feared her spell would let them eat and destroy everything useful to humanity. This would cause havoc to lots of innocent people. She realised that many other living things needed or wanted to eat the same things as humans. So if lots of these crocodiles were born, grew up and started wantonly eating all of that food, her magic would be hugely damaging to all sorts of other animals too.

The princess started to feel sick. She came to the stark conclusion that because it was impossible to stop all humans from acting badly, she had given those crocodile children permanent, magical powers of plundering. Desperately, she tried to retract her spell again and again.

The mermicorn in charge of her spell always appeared and said, "Your Royal Highness, I am sorry but you cannot change or cancel a permanent spell."

Eventually, the princess was left with no choice but her option of last resort. She had to confess her mess-up to her mother, the mermaid queen, and ask her for help.

The queen was not amused. Even worse, instead of the

queen shouting at her, she just stared at her daughter in silence before, after what seemed a very long time, she showered her with sarcastic pity and concern.

The queen, of course, knew that she could not change or cancel a permanent spell. The queen was an extremely thoughtful and smart monarch. She remembered a conversation that she had many years ago with an old retired lawyer. He told her that language was often the most powerful weapon anyone could have. He urged her to remember throughout her reign that words could carry a number of meanings. Therefore, the same words could be used by the queen in a variety of ways to do and mean a range of different things. He concluded by politely suggesting that sometimes her job would require her to explore the meanings of words and then persuade people to use them in the ways she wanted. The queen found that to be very sound advice and she had used it on a number of occasions during her reign. She resolved to apply this advice to her daughter's predicament.

The queen asked her daughter to write down the exact words of her spell. The princess was confused by this request, but she did not feel in any position to query it. She did as she was asked.

Her mother thanked her daughter and then sat staring at the words, almost without blinking, for what seemed a very long time. A smile spread across the queen's face. She leaned back in her chair.

"We need to chat with the mermicorn. How do I get to see her?" asked the queen.

"Well," her daughter started, "she seems to turn up every time I try to get rid of my spell."

"Brilliant plan," the queen stated gratefully.

Her daughter smiled weakly, feeling slightly better to have finally done something her mother liked.

The queen stood up, holding the written copy of her daughter's spell in her right hand, and stated aloud, "As Mermaid Queen, I am the only person whose magic is stronger than that of my daughter. I hereby revoke my daughter's spell, which she has copied here."

As she finished her spell, she waved the piece of paper in the air. That did the trick. The mermicorn appeared at once.

She looked a lot younger than the queen had expected. Her mermaid tail was strong, well-defined and flowed down to a large, powerful fin. It was the most vivid turquoise colour. Her unicorn top half was a striking, bold, black and white like a zebra's markings. She had a long rainbow-coloured mane. Her horn was sparkling gold with the occasional bright silver stars dancing around its point.

The mermicorn looked at the two royals before speaking directly to the mermaid queen, as it was she who had cast the forbidden spell, "Your Majesty, I regret to inform you that you cannot change or remove a permanent spell."

"Well," said the queen. "Surely as mermaid queen I can revoke any other mermaid's spell as part of my sovereign powers?"

"Your Majesty, you have sovereign powers in your realm here on Earth. Your powers do not extend to the magic spirit world. That is where spells exist. Sorry, Your Majesty, nice try, but it cannot be done. It's Rule 4 of the Mermaid and Mermicorn Royal Rules," said the mermicorn, whilst grinning a little cheekily at the queen.

"Well, you can't blame this earthly mermaid monarch trying it on a bit, can you?" laughed the queen. "Can I discuss a way forward with you, please? By the way, I hope you don't mind me asking, but what is your name?"

The mermicorn was taken aback by this response. In spite of her youthful appearance, she was not that new to her role. She had never dealt with royalty before this spell, but she had dealt with some mermaid aristocrats. Unfortunately, those aristocratic mermaids had not made a good impression with her. At first, she found them to be rather stiff, prim and proper, but at least they came across as quite nice and respectful. This only lasted until she told them something that they did not like. Then they showed their true colours and spoke to the mermicorn in a condescending manner, as if she was an inferior being and a nuisance. None of these aristocratic mermaids had ever had the courtesy to ask her about her name.

The mermaid princess had never been disrespectful to the mermicorn, but she had always been so upset and pre-occupied with her fears that they had never been able to have a real conversation. So this approach by the mermaid queen really impressed her.

"Thank you, Your Majesty. My name is Mary Mermicorn. I may be a spirit, but I prefer to be referred to as just a regular mermicorn, please."

"Of course, Mary. What a lovely name you have. It certainly suits you. However, I hope you don't mind me commenting but you are so splendid, so professional and so obviously intelligent, I would not dream of referring to you as just 'regular'. My name is Jane. Let's get rid of all the formalities, if that is all right with you? Shall we just use our first names as we chat about my problem, if that is all right with you?" asked the queen gently, using all of her regal flattery and charm.

The queen's manner worked. Mary was flabbergasted and blushed bright crimson with the gushing praise. She was certainly going to tell her mermicorn mates about this when she returned to the spirit realm. She knew they would be really impressed.

Beaming with happy surprise, Mary replied, "Yes, Your... I

mean, Jane. I agree it would be very nice to chat and use our first names. Thank you, you are very kind. I love my name and Jane is a really beautiful name too. Let's see if we can help each other."

The princess watched her mother's confident regal manner and genuinely pleasant nature in awe. She decided she would try to behave in a similar manner in future.

Mary and Jane chatted and joked like old friends. They started to pore over the piece of paper upon which the spell's words had been written. Mary listened to Jane's arguments that words could have many meanings and agreed with her points. They went into deep discussions about the spell and the principles to be applied in interpreting it. After many chocolate biscuits and cups of tea, Jane called over her daughter and let her know the results of their work.

Mary said that as long as the words of the permanent spell did not change, the Mermaid and Mermicorn Royal Rules did not stop the queen or princess telling her how they wanted the spell's words to be interpreted and applied. She continued that she would interpret and apply the spell as asked by them, if their request contained a reasonable meaning of the words, unless there was an exceptional reason not to do that.

As Mary was explaining all of this, the princess just stood, listened and hoped it could be sorted out. She kept clasping and unclasping her cold and sweaty hands in nervous anticipation. She noticed her mother and Mary standing up and winking at each other. They chatted loudly together about how the princess's spell could be interpreted in a number of different ways, but it was too vague to work out exactly what it meant. Therefore, it would really help Mary to do a proper job, if Jane could clarify what she was supposed to do to carry it out.

For a moment, the princess nearly ruined this agreed solution by getting rather indignant about the suggestion she did not cast a proper spell. Luckily, her mother noticed her daughter starting to get tetchy. Before she ruined the fruitful negotiations, Jane gave her a mother's stare. That worked. The princess just stood still and said nothing. Inwardly, she was still seething.

Mary and Jane agreed that this spell should have three reasonable clarifications.

Firstly, the spell's unique protections were agreed to mean they would make it difficult for humans to harm Crocky's daddy's children without exceptional reasons, they would make those children less attractive to being harmed by humans, and they would always be the least damaging and dangerous protections appropriate to the circumstances.

Secondly, plundering from humans was agreed to mean taking food grown or made for human consumption only.

Thirdly, as a failsafe to stop Crocky's daddy's children using the spell in completely unacceptable ways, if that ever were to happen, Mary would make any appropriate humans or animals aware so they could stop them, whilst still ensuring appropriate protections for those children from humans.

The deal was done. Jane and Mary, who were now most definitely new best friends, said their thanks to one another. They agreed to meet up regularly to check on how the spell was working and to catch up. Mary said her goodbyes to Jane and her daughter, before she disappeared back into the magical spirit realm.

As soon as Mary left, the princess ran over to her mother, hugged her tightly and sobbed her thanks. She vowed never to make permanent spells again – at least, without running it past her mother first!

Chapter Five

Crocky's Journey Into Captivity

Within a year of Crocky's daddy returning home from his Mediterranean experience, he had met and fallen in love with Crocky's mummy. After another year and a half, Crocky was born. It was then that Crocky's daddy spoke to his partner about his encounter with the mermaid princess and her strange spell. Crocky's mummy listened intently. At first, she was not sure if Crocky's daddy was telling the truth or if he was telling her a nice story. She stared into his eyes and it slowly dawned upon her that this was no joke. They chatted about what the spell could mean and decided against having any more children until they had worked it out. They spent the next nearly four years trying to do just that, before Crocky was orphaned on the eve of his fourth birthday.

The only magical effect that his parents thought they had worked out related to Crocky's size. At first, he grew like any other crocodile until he reached two feet long. Then he stopped growing. He was also quite slightly built and remained that way. His parents became very concerned. They consulted with their family doctor at the Lagoon Practice and followed Dr Snappy's advice to the letter. They altered his diet. They changed his exercise regime. They varied his sleeping times. Absolutely nothing worked to make a jot of difference to his shape or size.

It was then that Crocky's parents became convinced that his diminutive dimensions must have been caused by the mermaid princess's magic. However, they could not work out why. This made it difficult when they spoke with the young Crocky about it, so they just skirted around this issue.

Mary Mermicorn's logic was actually very simple. Humans would not want to eat a small crocodile or turn his skin into a fashion item because he was not big enough for this option to be cost effective. Humans would also not feel threatened by such a little creature. All Mary then needed to do was make sure that Crocky would never try to eat a human. Mary did this by planting in Crocky's mind the opinion that humans would taste disgustingly awful. This worked brilliantly. Crocky was never tempted to take even the smallest nibble!

As Crocky grew older, on many occasions as he went to bed, his daddy would tell and re-tell him the story of the mermaid princess. Crocky felt warm and comforted that he had something special that his brave father had won for him. He was told the story so often that he could remember all of it. After he lost his parents, Crocky kept reciting it to himself in his mind to help him remember these happy times with his daddy.

Immediately after he was orphaned, some human exotic animal smugglers picked him up. Mary's magic made sure he survived, but Mary looked on, aghast, when she saw these humans selling Crocky to an English exotic animal farm. That farm reared crocodiles and other creatures for their meat and skin. She watched him being transported there in a crate before being put into a small, single animal pen.

Crocky was taken there just before Easter and he remained at the farm until early January in following year. When he first arrived, poor Crocky was in a state of shock and deep, Inner distress. He had lost everything: his family, his home and his freedom.

Mary thought desperately how she could save him from these humans as the mermaid princess's spell demanded. She came up with this idea. Whilst he was asleep in the early hours of Maundy Thursday, Mary gave Crocky the ability to understand everything any human said, in whatever language they used. When he awoke, he watched the farm staff doing their morning chores and he could hear them chatting. Suddenly, he realised that these humans were not just making strange and meaningless groaning, moaning and grunting sounds. He could hear and understand everything they said. Crocky was astounded and could not quite believe what was going on. Over the hours and days, his surprise reduced and he realised how useful this skill was.

One of the first things he worked out was that some humans celebrated an event called Easter, which involved some decorations and eating lots of food, especially something called chocolate Easter eggs. Over the rest of the year, he saw that humans liked lots of celebrations, which usually involved some decorations and lots of food. At the end of the year, the humans enjoyed something really big called Christmas. So far as Crocky was concerned, many humans turned up the decorating and food eating to even greater levels. Crocky liked this aspect of humanity and wanted to join in.

Understanding human language also meant that Crocky found out what being at the farm would eventually mean to him. Whilst he had thought that he was at some risk, it was quite shocking to hear exactly what the humans intended to do to him. Nevertheless, Crocky soon worked out the meaning of the expression 'knowledge is power'. Now he knew what the humans intended, he could plan ways to survive, ably assisted by Mary.

Crocky learnt that humans loved small animals that could do tricks or looked cute. He also realised that if he could only get his head a bit higher up, he would be able to see and hear more of what the humans were saying and doing. He saw how some of the snakes at the farm were able to raise up their heads to see and hear better, even though they had no legs. He noticed that a number of humans seemed quite enchanted by this skill. Crocky had never seen any crocodile being able do anything like that, even though they had strong hind legs. He decided that there was no reason why he could not stand up on his back legs and raise his head like a snake. Mary thought that could help him against humans so she magicked that skill to him.

Initially, Crocky used the edge of his own pen to help him up. After a few wobbles, he found he could do it. He then practised standing up on his hind legs without support. When he perfected that, he moved to being able to walk. After a while swaying around like a sailor on a ship in a storm, he stabilised and became rather proficient at it. Once that was achieved, it did not take him long to be able to jog and run around on his hind legs.

Whilst he was doing all of this, the farm staff watched him in awe.

"He thinks he's a meerkat!" was the regular comment from the staff, but they loved him for it.

Crocky spotted this and realised his idea was working. He thought that this human appreciation could be really useful, but there was one big problem. His name was Perfidious Merchant: and he was the owner of this farm.

Perfidious did not find much amusing unless he was making money out of it. He was not bothered if he made money lawfully or not, just as long as he did.

He had two trusted, but equally dishonest, partners who helped him with the not-so-legitimate part of his business.

Robin Steele was a short and wiry man, who was a strong as an ox. He was in his mid-forties with receding grey hair. Perfidious and Robin were old friends, who had met through their passion for greyhound racing. Robin was able to source any animals from anywhere at amazingly inexpensive prices. He asked no questions about their origin and was even less bothered about it. He was the person who had bought Crocky from the crocodile poachers. He had worked with these men lots of times before. They even had their own secret, late night, rendezvous point within a nearby wooded clearing. The men would produce the stolen or poached animals, Robin would pay them in cash, and they would all go off quickly and quietly until the next time.

Ms Fi Sans was Perfidious' other key partner. She was a large, very stern, white-haired woman in her early sixties. She had been a teacher at a high school. During her teaching career, she had taught art, design, technology and computing. She was extremely smart and incredibly strict. Whether you were a student or a colleague, she insisted that everyone called her 'Ms' or 'Ms Sans'.

Her life as a teacher came to rather an abrupt end after she failed to get promotion to the post of deputy headteacher of her school. What particularly upset her was that the person who beat her to the job was the head of history, with whom she did not get along at all. Instead of looking for other job opportunities elsewhere, Ms Sans became involved in a most unfortunate misunderstanding with the money raised for a school history trip to Normandy. Instead of the money remaining in the school's bank account to be transferred to the travel company, it ended up in her bank account.

Needless to say, all of the various authorities were more than a little disappointed with Ms Sans. She ended up having an enforced career break for eighteen months at Her Majesty's Prison Widnes, and being barred from the teaching profession for life. HMP Widnes, though, was renowned for its rehabilitative approach to inmates. If offered lots of courses. As Ms Sans was a studious type, she spent a productive spell there learning new skills in printing, designing and computing. She left prison as the most proficient counterfeiter and computer hacker in the United Kingdom.

Perfidious had a number of contacts within a variety of prisons. Ms Sans came to his attention very quickly. He communicated with her through one of his prisoner friends and it was agreed that as soon as she left jail, she would start to work for Perfidious in a highly remunerated role.

Ms Sans's job was simple. Whenever Perfidious needed any paperwork or computer records to conceal his dodgy dealings, she would make forgeries or hack into any government or other computer systems to create or change records as required. She was brilliant at it. She never left any trace in any complete systems of her hacking. In Crocky's case, Ms Sans sorted out all the documentation and computer records needed to make his purchase look completely lawful.

Due to Crocky's size, Perfidious thought he was a lot younger than four years old. Therefore, he expected Crocky to grow very quickly at his farm. Perfidious only intended to keep Crocky for about eighteen months before he thought he would be large enough to be sold for his meat and skin. Perfidious expected to make a huge profit, but his plan was doomed from the outset thanks to Mary Mermicorn and the mermaid princess.

As much as he was fed, Crocky never grew or gained weight. As the weeks turned into months, Crocky could see and hear Perfidious getting more and more frustrated about this. Crocky's newly acquired skill to stand like a meerkat enabled him to get much better views to witness Perfidious' increasingly loud and angry comments. The more this happened, the more Crocky would smile to himself. Crocky was not the only one who found this rather amusing. Mary was watching Perfidious and finding his ill-tempered exasperation most entertaining.

As the year moved on into autumn, and the Christmas season was well and truly in the air, Perfidious had run out of patience with veterinary approved approaches trying to get Crocky to grow. He decided to move Crocky onto an extreme eating regime. He ordered his staff to replace all of Crocky's proper crocodile food with as much human food left-overs as they could. He told his workers that they had to focus on feeding Crocky as many highly calorific human food items as they could. The farm was situated in an area of England with high unemployment and few job opportunities. Perfidious threatened any member of staff with the sack if they failed to do as he ordered. He also promised to ensure that they would not find any other employment anywhere in their locality. His unpleasantness, wealth and contacts were such that no one doubted that Perfidious could and would do such a thing. His staff followed his orders, albeit very reluctantly.

As Christmas was coming, Crocky suddenly found himself

being fed roast turkey, pigs in blankets, roast potatoes, Christmas cake and puddings, all manner of chocolate treats and lots more besides. He had never tasted human food before. He found he loved it. Whenever the farm workers put this food into his pen, they saw him move faster than an Olympic sprinter to devour it in a very noisy flash.

SNAP, nom, nom, nom! And it was gone, right into Crocky's tummy.

At first, Perfidious watched the greedy little reptile wolf down this human food with malevolent pleasure and self-satisfaction at how clever his plan was. After a week of this, he ordered his staff to measure and weigh Crocky and tell him the results. The farm staff carried out this task as ordered. They looked at the scales and the tape measure and were stunned.

There was absolutely no change.

They re-measured him and re-weighed him.

Still no change.

They knew Perfidious would not be happy, so they emailed him the results with a suggestion that sometimes it took a few weeks before a change in diet took effect. That did not placate the nasty farm owner. He shouted so loudly and rudely when he saw their email that animals in the next county were covering their ears.

Perfidious ordered Crocky to be fed with even more food. Pastries, burgers, pizzas and all sorts of other higher calorie foods were given to him. Crocky was ecstatic about this turn of events.

SNAP, nom, nom, nom! went Crocky every time, finishing off all the food within a fraction of a second.

Every week he was measured and every week there was no difference in his weight or size. Crocky now understood another aspect of the mermaid princess's magic, and he loved it!

Mary watched all of this feeling very pleased with how the magic was working. The mermaid princess's spell meant that Crocky had an insatiable appetite for human food. However much the farm staff fed him, he never felt full or ill; and he never grew an inch anywhere on his body or put on a pound of weight.

Mary had come across people like Perfidious Merchant before. She knew that it was only a matter of time before Perfidious would get completely fed up with this situation because Crocky's enormous appetite was costing him so much money. When that happened, Mary knew that it could get very unpleasant for Crocky very quickly. As she had to keep him safe from humans, she made Crocky an escape plan of last resort. However, on the twelfth day of Christmas, that escape plan was no longer needed.

Chapter Six

Crocky Leaves the Farm

Most of the farm workers loved Crocky, his tricks and his antics. They enjoyed that he was the only creature they had ever come across who didn't do what Perfidious Merchant demanded; but they also knew how ruthless their boss was. Secretly, they decided that they had to find a way to get Crocky out of the farm before Perfidious removed him in a horrible way. Without Perfidious' knowledge, they recorded Crocky's meerkat impressions. On New Year's Day, they posted them on social media under the heading "HOME WANTED" with a contact phone number of their ringleader's best mate.

Mary noticed what they had done and looked around the UK, Ireland and beyond to see if anyone might want to buy Crocky and take him to safety. She came across the lovely owners of a small animal park in Cornwall, who were looking at giving a home to a suitable reptile. Mary made sure that the social media post kept popping up on their phones. These owners, Sam and Nik, were kind and thoughtful. They were very interested in Crocky and so phoned the number. The best mate explained Crocky's skills, his predicament, his size and the fact that he never grew. Sam and Nik were enchanted by the social media post and all of this information. They could not stand the thought of something bad happening to Crocky. They were also convinced that a small crocodile, who never grew any longer than two feet and who could stand on his hind legs like a meerkat, would be a great addition to their family-friendly park.

They attended the farm on the twelfth day of Christmas. The staff told Perfidious that they had potential buyers for Crocky, just before Sam and Nik arrived. Perfidious was very interested because he knew Crocky was costing him dearly and he was not worth much money at all due to his size.

Perfidious welcomed Sam and Nik. He used all of his boundless and insincere charm to drive the sale for as much cash as he could get. Whilst he told them about Crocky's tricks and the fact that he never grew, he conveniently 'forgot' to mention Crocky's never-ending appetite for human food. After some negotiation, and not believing his luck, Perfidious Merchant walked away from his chat with Sam and Nik with a cracking result for him – and an even better one for Crocky.

Before the day was over, Crocky was heading off to a nice new home in Cornwall, whilst Perfidious' food overheads plummeted and he had a large bundle of bank notes in his hands!

It was late in the evening when Crocky arrived at the animal park. Crocky was really happy to have been rescued from the farm, but he did have one regret. He knew that he was now going to be given ordinary crocodile food to eat again.

Yeuch! thought Crocky to himself at that prospect. *But I'd rather be condemned to eating disgusting 'official' crocodile food forever than have only a few more weeks of that yummy human stuff before being turned into a human dinner and fashion accessory!*

When he was placed into his new home, he gazed in amazement at its size and attractiveness. He had moved from a small pen area in a farm, where he knew exactly why Perfidious had bought him, to a wonderfully large covered area within what looked like a huge overarching greenhouse, where he would be safe.

In his new living area, Crocky had his own personal pond and an old walnut tree under which he could shelter and snooze. What was even better was his living space bordered a family dining section, which contained numerous tables and chairs. Beyond that dining zone, Crocky could clearly see a kitchen and serving area.

Of course, animal parks are frequented by large numbers of people, often families of all ages, who come to spend many enjoyable and educational hours seeing and learning about different species. Whilst visiting, many people enjoy meals and snacks. This animal park was no different.

In this animal park, the presence of a small, cute, green crocodile, who could stand on his back legs like a meerkat, next to the family eating area, became a massive visitor attraction very quickly. Crocky could see and smell all of this yummy human food so tantalisingly close to him. He knew humans loved his meerkat-like tricks, so he wondered if he could charm and entertain the human visitors into giving him some of their food.

As soon as the park opened in the morning and the first human visitors arrived, Crocky's food-driven plan clicked into action. It was not long before visitors started to move their dining tables and chairs right next to his enclosure's four and a half feet tall fencing so they could get a better view of his antics whilst they ate. As the tables were now adjoining his home, the human food placed on them was very close to him as well. Crocky saw this. He started willing it to come to him. All of this scrumptious food was now only a foot or so away.

"So near and yet so far," mused Crocky in utter frustration.

This carried on until the autumn. Crocky had never given up hope and his perseverance finally paid off. One bright and breezy October lunchtime, Crocky was doing his meerkat sentry guard impression when a visitor came to a table, which was virtually touching the fence to Crocky's area. The visitor brought with him a plate upon which was a massive and piping hot Cornish pasty. He put the plate down on the table to let it cool slightly before he tucked in. The visitor decided to take a photograph of Crocky. He wanted a particular angle for his picture, which he could only get by leaning quite far over the top of the fencing. Unfortunately for this visitor, his leaning skills were not as proficient as his photography abilities. He lost his balance and, in a bit of a panic, he grabbed out striking the table hard. This resulted in a violent and sudden tipping of this piece of dining furniture, causing his pasty to be jettisoned over the fencing into Crocky's enclosure.

This was the answer to Crocky's prayers and dreams. The pasty landed with a thud just a yard away from him. At lightning speed, Crocky shot over to it.

SNAP, nom, nom, nom!

Within a fraction of a second, the pasty had gone into Crocky's tummy. It was love at first bite. From that moment, he resolved to not eat 'official' crocodile food any more – unless there was no alternative.

The visitor and all the other humans, who saw what had happened, were stunned. They were then mightily amused and impressed by Crocky's speed and eating ability. Laughter started to fill the building. A toddler, who had seen what Crocky had done and who also found it highly amusing, was handed an ice cream cone. It contained the most gloriously delicious scoops of vanilla ice cream made from the finest Cornish clotted cream. Protruding proudly out of the top of this sweet delight was a deeply embedded flaky piece of finest chocolate. This treat sent the toddler into a state of hyper-excitement. She threw her head and arms about with such force that her whole ice cream flew out of her grasp and into Crocky's enclosure. Crocky was at the ice cream in a flash.

SNAP, nom, nom, nom!

More laughter echoed around the building.

A trend had now started. This was very naughty. People should not feed farm, park or zoo animals human food. It can make them very ill. Crocky could only eat it because of the mermaid princess' magic – and he was and is the only animal anywhere who was blessed with that magic.

However, over the next hours and days ,more human found its way into Crocky's home.

There was strawberry jelly...

SNAP, nom, nom, nom!

There were cakes...

SNAP, nom, nom, nom!

There were sandwiches, biscuits, crisps, chips... you name it, and it ended up in Crocky's area.

SNAP, nom, nom, nom!

Every time without fail, all gone into his tummy in the blink of an eye.

By now the food was not accidentally falling into his enclosure at all. The speed and joy of this meerkat-mimicking small crocodile, who could devour all kinds of human food in an instant, made Crocky a firm favourite. Crocky was overjoyed by his good fortune; but, sadly, good luck sometimes does not last.

The animal park's owners, Sam and Nik, were extremely caring and responsible people. They knew that crocodiles should not be fed like this. They were tearing their hair out trying to think of ways to stop people giving Crocky food. They tried signs imploring visitors not to feed Crocky. They tried staff standing by his enclosure, but some naughty people kept feeding him.

Sam and Nik kept Crocky under constant health checks due to the amount and types of human food he was eating – particularly as he was not touching his proper food. They, and the park's vets, were astounded that regardless of what he ate, or how much he ate, he was always in absolutely tip-top medical condition. In fact, they were so astonished they arranged with a local university's veterinary department to carry out a study on him.

However, Sam and Nik were not the only people who were deeply concerned about Crocky's diet. One of those people made an anonymous phone call to a national UK animal charity claiming that Crocky was being mistreated by being fed improperly. That charity called in an undercover veterinary inspector, who visited the park in early November. She saw how Crocky was being fed by the public, she saw what he was eating, she saw the huge amounts of human food he was eating and she then filed an official complaint to the park's local authority, West Tamar Valley Council.

Within twenty-four hours of that visit, the council put an end to Crocky's alimentary joy. They ordered that the fencing around his enclosure had to be changed to make it impossible for anyone to be able to get human food to Crocky. Sam and Nik were told that the park would be closed down if they did not do this immediately. This left Sam and Nik with no alternative. At significant expense, they had to get these alterations done at once. The result was the construction of a twenty-feet-high, transparent, super-tough, shatter-proof wall of glass between Crocky and the dining area. All of the dinner tables were moved at least six feet away from the enclosure's new glass perimeter wall. No words can describe how upset this made Crocky.

To make matters worse for his mood, this change happened just as the animal park started its main Christmas menu, including a whole range of festive nourishment. Crocky had been looking forward to this so much, but now all of these tummy treats had been taken away from him.

He was livid that no human had bothered to ask his opinion about any of this. Whilst he accepted that humans might have a problem understanding his Crocodilian language, even with his newly acquired Cornish accent, he could not comprehend why they had not waited for the university study to happen and report its results. He had heard various discussions about this piece of academic work and so he knew all about it. He was quite happy to carry on eating human food in vast quantities to help the research – and his greedy self! – safe in the knowledge that the mermaid princess's magic would have ensured that he would always be fine. He was certain that the study would have produced results to prove to everyone that he could continue eating at this prodigious level without any health problems, but the council's demand had changed all of that. He recognised that the study was not going to happen now. He knew that, henceforth, he was going to be condemned to eating what he regarded as yucky 'official' crocodile food only, unless he could come up with some way to get around this problem.

Crocky decided that he would sulk for as long as it took for the humans to realise the error of their ways and let him eat human food again. As part of this sulking exercise, he refused to do his meerkat impressions any more. He just lay in the pool in his enclosure like a little log. He would only eat 'official' crocodile food when his hunger became so unbearable that he could hold out no longer. This decision did not help Crocky's mood or change his situation. He would lay watching the human visitors munching their roast turkey dinners and other Christmas treats and compare it to what he had to eat.

Look at all of those humans tucking into their lovely food, Crocky would think to himself forlornly, *and just compare it to the "goodness-knows-what-disgustingness" they have given me to eat. It really is not fair; not fair at all!*

Crocky sulked and sulked. To this, he added a determination to end his misery. He vowed that when he succeeded, he would more than make up for lost food. He kept his sulk pose, but instead of wallowing in negative thoughts about food, he was thinking, scheming and plotting.

Mary Mermicorn watched Crocky's behaviour. She wondered if the mermaid princess' spell allowed her to intervene.

Not yet, she thought. *There's nothing wrong with proper crocodile food. Just because he prefers human food does not mean he should be fed it. I prefer magic rainbow sweets, but it would do me no good if I just ate them all the time!*

Sam and Nik were also trying to work out what to do. Crocky's sudden change in behaviour made them very worried in case he was seriously ill. They called in the park's vets, who checked him over. After completing many tests, the vets concluded that there was nothing physically wrong with Crocky at all.

When Sam and Nik read the veterinary report, Sam turned to Nik and said, "You know, Nik, if our crocodile were a human, I'd say he was sulking!"

Nik nodded in reply. "I was thinking exactly the same thing, Sam."

Sam and Nik certainly knew their animals.

Chapter Seven

Chookoo Squirrel

Christmas and the New Year came and went. The lights and glitter of the festive period gave way to dark and bleak days. Cornwall and the rest of south-west England were lashed with one Atlantic storm after another. The local wild animals began to suffer as their food stores and resources were battered and washed away.

Chookoo Squirrel was one of those unlucky creatures. He was the last red squirrel in his Cornish valley. He thought he had been very clever putting his nut stores along a nearby river bank. He had placed a pile of his food under every third tree, so he could remember where they were. Unfortunately, the incessant wind and rain eventually caused the river to flood and mud slides to cascade down the hillsides. His hoards of nuts were completely wiped out.

He was left in a desperate plight, searching and begging for sustenance without much success. By February, he was barely getting a meal's worth of food a week from anywhere. The final straw snapped in late February. In the pitch evening darkness, the worst storm of the winter brought down his tree house, including the whole, once mighty, oak tree in which he had built it.

He scrambled out of the wreckage of his home. It was irreparable. He trudged away trying to find some shelter and food, growing progressively weaker by the hour. Cold, tired and feeling his situation was hopeless, he reached a quiet, muddy and potholed country lane seemingly in the middle of nowhere. He looked up at the heavens. The storm had passed but dawn had revealed a miserable, grey, leaden sky. Chookoo sat down on a slight stony mound in the middle of the lane and sighed. His seat was not very comfortable, but it was slightly drier than the muddy and waterlogged land around. He closed his eyes trying to think of any solution.

To his surprise, a mermicorn popped into his thoughts. He opened his eyes and she was still there. He stood up rapidly in shock.

It was Mary Mermicorn. Events had moved on in the animal park. They meant that Mary had changed her mind. The mermaid princess's spell now required her to help Crocky. She could see that Chookoo needed help too. As she was a kindly mermicorn, this created the perfect opportunity to help two animals at once. Since her chat with the mermaid queen, she knew that she could help out anyone else as long as she was carrying out the spell. So that is what Mary decided to do.

Mary spoke to Chookoo, "Hi, I'm Mary. I'm a mermicorn visiting you from the magical spirit kingdom. I know this sounds very odd, but it's true. Don't worry, I'm really here. You're not dreaming. I know you're tired, wet and hungry. Please just keep going down this lane and you will be fine. I will give you the energy you need. Hurry."

Mary vanished. In spite of her words, Chookoo was still not sure if he was dreaming or if Mary was real. Suddenly, he felt a surge of energy throughout his body that caused him to jump. His mind was then filled with hope. He thought he had nothing to lose but to keep on going down the lane. He hopped around the corner at speed. He looked ahead and stopped in shock. Straight in front of him was the animal park.

"My goodness, I wasn't just dreaming about that mermicorn. Where there are animals, there will be food and shelter," cried Chookoo in joyous relief. "Thank you, Mary, for saving me!"

He rushed to the animal park. There was a ten feet tall wall around it, but that was no trouble for a hungry and wet squirrel, who saw his salvation on the other side of it. He climbed over the wall with ease. As he landed inside the grounds of the animal park, he saw a number of large buildings ahead of him. He went over to the nearest one and noticed a narrow ventilation hole. His lack of food had made him painfully thin. This meant he was able to squeeze himself through this very small aperture into the dry and warm interior. As he exited this opening and stood up, he saw ahead of him an old, gnarled walnut tree with lots of ungathered walnuts all over the floor.

"Thank you!" Chookoo squeaked out loud.

He knew that there could not be any other squirrels around as they would never have left all those walnuts just lying there.

He looked about him, nervously flicking his tail. He saw he was in an enclosure within a much larger greenhouse-type building. No one seemed to be there. He was sure no one was there. He was alone with his feast! He prepared to tuck in. Just as he bent down to bite deeply into the largest walnut of the lot, a strong, green and scaly foot flattened him to the floor with a splat!

Crocodiles are great at hiding. Sulking, hungry, always watchful, scheming, two-feet-long crocodiles, though, are the best.

A gruff voice came from above Chookoo, "Oi, *SNAP*, what's your game?"

Chookoo had, of course, unwittingly stumbled into Crocky's home. No squirrel was ever going to go foraging in a crocodile enclosure – not even that of such a small snapper – unless they did not have a clue of its occupant.

"D–ddd–don't eat me!" Chookoo stammered in terror. "Please don't eat me."

"I've no intention of eating you," snapped Crocky.

His first thoughts were that this intruder was so thin and scrawny he would not make a good meal; and he was not even cooked! He decided that no squirrel would be there unless they were very silly or desperate. Looking at Chookoo's state, he presumed the latter.

"What's your name?" Crocky demanded.

"Chookoo," croaked out the prone squirrel.

"Chookoo? That's a really unusual name, if you are telling the truth," probed Crocky, starting to show his teeth at the squirrel.

Chookoo started to gabble as fast as he could, "My dad wanted to call me Cyril. My mum wanted to call me Horatio. They wouldn't agree, even after I was born, so I had no name for weeks. Then, as a baby squirrel, I heard a cuckoo in the woods and tried to copy her sound. As I was so small, I didn't get it quite right. I would say 'chookoo' instead of 'cuckoo'. My parents were so amused and enchanted by this, they ended their argument and named me Chookoo. When my sister was born, my parents had stopped these silly disputes and agreed to call her Simone. So I was the only one with the unusual name."

Crocky thought about this answer for a moment. He thought that it was so bizarre, it must be true.

Crocky carried on with his questioning, "What's your game? I won't ask again, SNAP!"

"I'm sorry, sir! I didn't realise this was your tree. I was

desperate. These storms. I've lost my home. Lost my food. Lost everything. Have mercy!" Chookoo babbled at top speed.

Then Crocky had an idea; or more accurately, Mary Mermicorn put an idea into his brain.

Crocky understood what it felt like to lose your food and this squirrel could be really useful. Squirrels were great climbers. Squirrels were great at picking up and holding things. Squirrels were great at solving problems. Squirrels would often do lots for food. A sneaky, toothy grin spread over his face.

"I've no intention of eating you as long as you help me," said Crocky menacingly.

He put his teeth within a squirrel's fur breadth of Chookoo's face and licked his lips extravagantly, hoping his bad acting skills would not let him down.

They didn't. The terrified tree hopper would do anything to avoid those teeth.

"Of, of, of course, sir!" stuttered the terrified squirrel.

Crocky had never been called 'sir' before and he had been called it twice now in less than a minute. Crocky was a down-to-earth type of crocodile and that was not his style.

"There's no need to call me 'sir'. I'm Crocky. That's a good chap. Have a walnut," said Crocky in a much less threatening and more relaxed manner.

Crocky used his tail to flick the walnut that he had seen Chookoo trying to eat. That huge juicy nut rolled just in front of the prone squirrel's face. Crocky lifted his foot off Chookoo and allowed the squirrel to get up. Chookoo scrambled warily to his feet.

"Go on, eat. You looked like you need it," said Crocky, beckoning to the walnut with his head

Chookoo did not need another invitation. He bent down in a flash and started stuffing his cheeks with that huge walnut. No nut had ever tasted so nice before.

Crocky continued, "I have no interest in walnuts, unless they are encased in chocolate or crushed into walnut cakes. You look starving, cold and wet. Stay a while. Fill your boots with walnuts, but in return will you help me, please?"

Chookoo momentarily stopped his munching. He was not expecting this! He'd heard that all crocodiles were scary. He had been told by many that they were just walking and swimming eating machines, who cared for no one but themselves and filling their tummies. However, this crocodile was now being nice to him. He had not tried to eat him. In fact, he had done the opposite. He was helping him in his hour of need. He was even asking for Chookoo's help – politely!

"Of course, Crocky. What do you want?" asked Chookoo,

before quickly going back into munching mode.

Crocky spoke with Chookoo about all of his problems at the animal park. He told Chookoo that he wanted to escape as soon as possible, but there was no way he could get out on his own. He stared pleadingly at Chookoo as he told him that Chookoo's squirrel abilities would allow him to get his freedom. Crocky promised that he would let Chookoo stay in his area and have exclusive access to all of the walnuts there in return for him using his climbing, grabbing and problem-solving skills to help Crocky to escape. Once they had sprung Crocky's release, the small reptile promised Chookoo that he would help him for as long as he wanted on the outside until they were both safe and decided to go their separate ways. Crocky then told Chookoo that if he agreed in principle to help him on those terms, he would provide full details of his escape plan that evening.

Free walnuts, a warm and dry place to stay, help to find a permanent new home, and not being eaten by Crocky were more than enough reasons for Chookoo to accept this generous offer.

The deal was agreed.

Chapter Eight

New Staff at the Animal Park

What had made Crocky certain that he needed to leave the animal park and had also persuaded Mary to help him to flee? The answer lay in the arrival of two new members of staff and their appalling behaviour.

At the start of February, Dan and Stan joined the park's evening shift. Their jobs were to clean and close down Crocky's building, with the exception of the kitchen area, which was already locked and alarmed. Whilst the animal park's owners and all other staff were kind, honest and conscientious, these two people were not like that at all.

At 17.00 each day, the kitchen stopped serving the public. It was then cleaned and closed down by the catering staff. When they had finished, they would lock up the kitchen and set its alarm. The animal park, though, stayed open to the public until 18.00. At about 18.30, Dan and Stan would enter Crocky's building and go to the key cabinet at the back of the dining area. They would take out two keys, which were on a single key ring with a bright green fob. Those keys opened the two doors that led into Crocky's enclosure. Crocky could see one of those doors at the back of his living area. This door led into a small rectangular holding zone. The second door also opened into that holding place, but that one led to the outside.

Dan and Stan would use those keys to open both doors,

come into Crocky's enclosure, check it, sort out any food and water for him for the night and do any necessary cleaning. They did not do the job very well. Whilst they were in his enclosure, Crocky would lie in his pool motionless, watching and listening.

Dan and Stan had heard about what had happened to Crocky and how his human food treats had been stopped. They thought it was very funny. When they were in his enclosure, they would mock him. They weren't scared of a two-feet-long crocodile, whom they never saw moving.

Dan would say to Crocky, "I bet you're hungry now you can't get any food from the kitchen. I bet you wish you could get out of here into the kitchen. But you're not allowed. You're too small and stupid to do anything about it."

Stan would join in this bullying too.

Stan would say, "Yeh, too small and stupid. We're not allowed in the kitchen either, but we are big and clever. We know how the alarms work and where the keys are kept. We know how to turn the CCTV on and off. We've been nicking food and drink from our last two jobs, but we always leave before anyone finds out. The bosses of all of these places are too stupid and trusting to even dream of what we're up to!"

Throughout this horrible behaviour, Dan and Stan would laugh and cackle like evil witches. They would even cruelly sing to Crocky,

"Would you like some food from the kitchen tonight?

Would you like some food from the kitchen tonight?

Would you like some food from the kitchen tonight?

Well, you can't,

Because it's ours!"

They would finish singing with a snigger. They would follow this up with numerous pretend-eating sounds as if they were devouring a large meal.

Crocky just lay still. He saw, heard and understood everything. So did Mary Mermicorn.

At about 19,00 each night, which was when Dan and Stan would finish their actual work, they would leave and lock up the two doors that have access to the back of Crocky's enclosure and return to the dining area. Instead of putting the two crocodile enclosure keys into the key cabinet, they would drop them onto a table. They would then turn off the building's CCTV cameras and the activated parts of the alarm system.

The alarm system had various zones. When the kitchen was closed and locked before 18.00 by the catering staff, that locking would automatically set the kitchen's alarm. Similarly, the locking of both doors to the crocodile enclosure automatically set the alarm for that area. However, when anyone turned off any alarms in the building, the system automatically turned off all alarms for all zones. It was a peculiarity of that system designed to stop alarms being set off by accident.

After Dan and Stan had switched off the CCTV and alarms, they would go to the key cabinet, take out the kitchen key, open the kitchen door, start playing music on a mobile phone very loudly, and help themselves to drink and various bits of scrumptious food. Crocky would hear their laughing, dancing, eating and drinking as he lay in his pool. Mary Mermicorn saw and heard what they were doing too.

After about fifteen minutes, they would come out of the kitchen, lock its door, put the kitchen key back into the key cabinet, turn the CCTV and alarms back on, pick up the crocodile enclosure keys from the table, put those keys away in the key cabinet, lock that cabinet, and then they would leave the whole building in very good moods.

As they left, they would often mutter to Crocky quietly, but loud enough for him to hear, "We've just eaten your old food. Very nice. Shame you can't have it any more."

This seemed to add to their horrible enjoyment.

Crocky just lay there. He saw, heard and understood everything. So did Mary Mermicorn.

This made Crocky extremely upset and very angry.

Crocky would think to himself, *How dare they eat that food? It should be going into my tummy and making money for the animal park to keep the other animals and me happy, safe and well. At least when I used to get it, visitors had bought it to fund our homes here!*

Dan and Stan had no idea that Crocky could understand English. They also had no idea that they were seriously annoying a mermicorn, who was tasked by magic to protect Crocky from humans. What they were doing was causing Crocky ever-increasing mental anguish. What they were doing was mean, selfish and cruel. What they were doing was harming the animal park and all of the animals there – not just Crocky. Dan and Stan were doing it deliberately. They did not intend to stop. They did not care.

Mary did care. She cared lots. She was livid with them. She decided Crocky needed to be protected from them and their behaviour. Unwittingly, Dan and Stan persuaded Mary to help Crocky to escape.

Chapter Nine

Crocky's Escape

Mary popped a sly thought into Crocky's mind about Dan and Stan a few days before Chookoo turned up. It was, *Maybe their greed can help me.*

Over the next few nights, Mary placed a number of dreams into Crocky's head. They explained in exact detail how he could escape and what to consider.

Thanks to Mary, Crocky realised that the high transparent wall that separated him from the dining area did not go all the way up to the glass roof at the top of the main building. This meant that there was a gap between the wall and the roof. One of the branches of the walnut tree was slightly higher than the top of the wall. It was so long that had the wall gone all the way up to the roof, the tip of the branch would have rested against it.

The wall of glass was quite thick, so it was wide enough to enable any small animal to walk along it. This barrier also continued to the outer wall of the main building. As the main building was built like a huge greenhouse, it had a considerable metal framework from top to bottom. This provided a climbing frame effect for any animals who might be around and want to try it out. Crocky just needed to find a creature who could climb up the tree, go along this branch, hop onto the top of the wall, climb down the building's frame and be able to do the reverse journey with the doors' keys very quickly and without being spotted.

Mary had the answer: a squirrel. Squirrels are incredible climbers and problem solvers. They can be really fast and their ability to pick things up is legendary. Mary just had to find the right squirrel. Chookoo was the one.

Chookoo had turned up in Crocky's enclosure shortly before the morning staff arrived. As soon as Crocky saw him, he knew, thanks to Mary's help, that Chookoo was his chance for freedom.

After they had made their deal, Crocky warned Chookoo that the morning staff would be arriving at any moment. He asked him to hide in a hole towards the top of the walnut tree and watch everything.

Chookoo agreed and made himself at home there. He had a wonderfully clear vantage point view over the whole building. He was more than happy because it was warm and dry. He had also taken up some walnuts to munch on quietly during the day. No one noticed he was there, just as Crocky wanted.

That evening, Dan and Stan turned up as usual. As ever, they cleaned Crocky's enclosure to a bad standard, whilst they subjected him to more ridicule and bullying. They followed their routine of locking the two doors leading from his enclosure, putting the keys down on the table, turning off the CCTV and alarms, taking the kitchen key, going into the kitchen and having a bit of a party there. As Dan and Stan were helping themselves in the kitchen, Crocky called Chookoo down from his hole and gave him half a dozen more large walnuts.

"You see what I've had to put up with, Chookoo. Every day this happens without fail. And yes, they are stealing from the kitchen at the moment. I can't put up with this any more. I need to get out of here," sighed Crocky.

"They are unbelievably unpleasant, Crocky. I can really see why you need to get out of here as soon as possible. I will help you in any way I can. You saved my life. It's the least I can do. You are my friend," stated Chookoo with a friendly smile.

Crocky grinned back. He pointed up the walnut tree.

"Can you see that two-feet-long branch up there?" asked Crocky. "It's the one which is almost dangling off the trunk. It must be five or six feet up."

Chookoo looked up and nodded.

"Be a good sport and chew it off please?" continued Crocky.

Chookoo didn't need asking twice. He shot off and gnawed away the last few woody sinews connecting the branch to the tree. It fell to the floor with a bang. Dan and Stan were oblivious to all of this. Their music was far too loud and their concentration was so elsewhere that Chookoo could have exploded a huge firework and they would never have noticed.

When Chookoo returned to his friend, he saw that Crocky was standing next to the fallen branch. Crocky flicked his tail and propelled the detached piece of tree into his pond. It landed with a gentle splash into Crocky's usual sulking spot.

"Hey, Crocky, from a distance it looks a bit like you in the pond there," joked Chookoo.

Crocky sniggered and replied, "Exactly. That's the point. I'll lie on it now and through tomorrow. I will scrape a few of my scales onto it to make it look even more like me. When we leave tomorrow night, those two will never notice the difference. All they care about is being nasty and stealing. Now listen to this, please. I said this morning that we would discuss my escape plan this evening. This is the time. I say we escape tomorrow night when they are in the kitchen. What do you think?"

Chookoo smiled back. The pair put their heads together, discussed and agreed exactly how they would escape together in under ten minutes. This gave them enough time to return to their previous positions before Dan and Stan came out of the kitchen.

As those two staff members left the building, they didn't even bother to glance towards Crocky as they made their nasty farewell comments about him. Crocky just lay in the pond. He was motionless in body, but his mind was racing.

The next evening seemed to take an age to come. Crocky and Chookoo did not move all day. Crocky lay on the branch and Chookoo hid in the hole in the tree.

When the evening arrived, Dan and Stan turned up as usual. They worked and behaved in exactly the manner Crocky and Chookoo expected.

As they did so, a single thought kept repeating in Crocky's mind, *Just you wait!*

The time came when Dan and Stan left Crocky's enclosure. He heard them closing and locking the two doors behind him. He waited and saw them come into view in the dining area ahead of him.

Yes! thought Crocky, as he saw the keys being dropped onto the table.

Result! declared Crocky's mind, as he saw the CCTV and alarm systems being turned off.

Crocky held his breath as he watched Dan and Stan go into the kitchen, close the door behind them and start their fifteen minutes of thieving and music playing.

Splash! went Crocky's tail as he slapped it down into the water behind him as loudly as he could. That was the signal to the hiding Chookoo that the escape was on!

Chookoo was hiding inside the tree's trunk waiting for this moment. He heard Crocky's tail crash into the surface of his pond as clear as a bell. In an instant, he jumped out of his hole and shot up the tree. He scampered along the branch, which stopped near to the top of the glass barrier to Crocky's enclosure. Upon reaching the end of this branch, he did his favourite flying squirrel leap onto the top of the glass. He landed with a small thud, grasping the edges of the transparent wall with his sharp, strong claws. He used his bushy tail to provide him with the necessary extra balance as he held himself firm.

Crocky was watching from below and let out a gasp. His heart was beating loudly in his throat and butterflies were doing somersaults in his tummy.

Mary was also taking a keen interest in these events. She was a lot more relaxed than Crocky. If anything went wrong with this escape effort, she was ready to step in and help – and she had all of the magic anyone could need to make sure the escape plan worked.

Chookoo raced along the top of the wall to where it met the large exterior windows of the main building. Those windows were held together by a very strong metal framework, which ran from the floor to the roof. He jumped onto this metallic skeleton and used a mixture of sliding and hopping to lead him safely and rapidly all the way down to the floor as if it was a steep, zig-zagging, silvery pathway to the ground.

As soon as he reached terra firma, he sprinted to the table where the enclosure keys lay unattended. He sprung up and grabbed them. He put them between his extremely strong teeth, turned around and did the reverse journey back into Crocky's enclosure with such skill and speed that Crocky had to use all of his willpower not to cry out and clap his feet in glee.

Within three minutes, the squirrel was back in the enclosure, jumping off the base of the tree and racing to the first door that led to Crocky's freedom. As he reached the door, Chookoo thought of a problem.

"Which key?" murmured Chookoo to himself, slightly perplexed. "No time to work it out properly. I know. Let's try the shinier one!"

Mary knew that Chookoo preferred brighter things, so she let him think that the correct key was a bit more sparkly than the other one. This piece of magic worked a treat. Chookoo put the key into the door. It unlocked with a click and without any problem. The door opened easily.

Overjoyed, the squirrel raced through to the second door. This area was rather dark but Chookoo had very good eye-sight. He put the second key straight into the keyhole, turned it, and with a clunk this door opened with no difficulty.

He looked around triumphantly. He was surprised to see Crocky already next to him with the widest toothy grin of satisfaction and joy. Crocky shot past Chookoo, out of the second door and threw himself into a nearby holly bush to hide.

Crocky stifled an "Ouch" in the back of his throat as the prickly bush spiked him in places where nobody should be pronged.

Crocky then whispered to Chookoo through teeth gritted in pain, "Log's in place, my dear friend, *SNAP!* You have about eight minutes to get those keys back to the table and join me here with both doors closed behind you. Hurry and good luck!"

With the speed of a gazelle being chased by a pride of lions, Chookoo turned and shot off. He skidded, he slid, he screeched, but only six minutes later he had completed his mission and was safely outside the two closed doors.

In his haste, Chookoo had accidentally dropped the doors' keys back onto the table rather than placed them quietly as he had intended. Fortunately for him, the clattering of the keys was more than drowned out by Dan and Stan's indescribably awful and extremely loud singing along to a famous old song that they were playing on their phone, as they continued their thieving and naughty fun in the kitchen.

Mary was watching throughout. She noticed that the keys had not been returned to the same spot where Dan and Stan had left them. She considered this error but she formed the view that they were near enough in the right place that Dan and Stan would never notice. Therefore, she left Chookoo to race back to Crocky rather than put the thought into Chookoo's head to go back and replace them exactly as he had found them.

"We're free!" exclaimed Chookoo, whilst catching his breath beside Crocky's temporary holly bush hiding spot.

"*Shhh.* Not yet," whispered Crocky. "Quick, hide in here."

Crocky dragged Chookoo into the holly bush with him. Chookoo did not appreciate the spikes and let out a strangled squeak of discomfort.

They waited motionlessly, which was not that hard because any movements were rather painful. They watched Dan and Stan come out of the building and lock it, which set all of the building's alarms. As Dan and Stan walked happily away, they were even joking about how lazy Crocky was, and how he never moved from his position in the pond.

Crocky and Chookoo heard them. They were pleased that the log trick in the pond had worked but this reminder of these humans' unpleasantness added to their determination to complete the escape.

Once they were sure that Dan and Stan had gone, Crocky whispered, "Right, Chookoo. You see that stream there? The one which flows through this park. That is my way out. You can hitch a lift on my back, if you want, or you can use the squirrel way over the wall. It's your choice."

"I'll take the wall. I don't like water very much. It's, well, too wet!!" joked Chookoo in a quietly spoken reply.

The friends chuckled, but they soon stopped because this caused the holly bush to move and scratch them again all over. The pain was now too much for Crocky. He was sure there were no humans left in the animal park, so the coast was clear for the next part of their escape – and he wanted to end his discomfort as soon as possible!

Crocky bolted out of the bush and called to Chookoo behind him, "See you over the other side. Last one there's a silly sausage!"

Chookoo wasn't expecting such a sudden burst of energy from his friend. He watched Crocky dive headfirst into the swollen, fast-flowing stream and away to freedom.

"Oi!" Chookoo called after Crocky. "Races should begin 'On your marks, set, go'. I'll get you for that blatant cheating!"

Chookoo bounded out of his hiding place and shot up the park's outer wall trying to catch up with Crocky. His slim chances of winning the race ended on the wall due to the large amounts of slippery moss and ivy over it, which required very careful navigation.

As he slid down the other side, Chookoo saw the stream had overflown its banks with all the storm water. He peered along its flooded route and spotted what looked like a fallen branch about a hundred yards ahead of him partly concealed within some reeds and longer grasses.

The branch then blinked and shouted across to him, "I see you're the silly sausage. Lucky for you, I've run out of ketchup as I only like my sausages with that yummy red sauce, *SNAP!*"

Chookoo raced over to his friend and replied laughingly, "If I'm a silly sausage, you're a cheating chipolata! Good journey, Crocky?"

Crocky grinned back. "Not bad. Dealt with a bully on the way. There was this massive pike hiding in the stream as it went under the wall. Full of his own self-importance, he was. He saw me in the gloom and must have thought I was a frog or something. He shot in front of me and showed me his choppers saying, 'Prepare to be dinner!' I know pike can swim quickly but all I did was give him a nice big smile – and I might have shown him a few of my gnashers... He must have nearly broken the sound barrier as he fled! *Tee hee hee hee!* He shot off so fast he's probably reached the French coast by now. *SNAP! Ha ha ha! SNAP!*"

Crocky continued, whilst still chortling to himself, "There's a small town down this stream. Let's head off there for some sleep and food. I'm starving!"

"Good idea," replied Chookoo. "My mate Suki lives down there. She'll see us all right."

With that, the two friends skipped off together in high spirits, just as it started to rain again.

Chapter Ten

Suki Cat and Ella Eagle

Suki was a huge and cuddly ball of ginger and white fur. She was the Trelawny family cat. The Trelawny family were the local town butchers and bakers. Their premises comprised two adjoining shops at the northern end of the Main Street. There was an old, large and unevenly paved courtyard immediately behind those shops, around which were a number of other Trelawny family business buildings including a bakery, a kitchen and a barn. Suki had a free run of the whole site. She was much loved by family and customers alike – and even better fed. She was extremely friendly and hospitable. She was completely down-to-earth and she had a heart of gold.

It was very late in the evening when Crocky and Chookoo arrived at the Trelawny's premises. The town was a lot further down the stream than Crocky had expected, so when they finally reached their destination, they were soaking wet and starving. Chookoo knocked on an oversized catflap that led into the courtyard. Both animals had large raindrops dripping from their noses.

They waited. In the distance, they heard pawsteps, which became louder and heavier until a huge smiling face popped out of the catflap.

"Chookoo, my dear friend. So nice to see you. What brings you here? Come in, come in. You're soaking wet. You'll catch your death of cold out there. And welcome to your friend. Any friend of my Chookoo is a friend of mine. Come in. Come in." Suki spoke and fussed with a jolly light voice delivered at superfast speed.

Crocky smiled to himself and thought, *Suki talks nearly as fast as Chookoo did when we first met – under my foot!*

Chookoo and Crocky entered the courtyard and were shown into a building on the far left-hand side. As soon as they entered, they were struck by the fantastic colours, smells and warmth within. They had been taken into an enormous kitchen. Crocky and Chookoo thought it was a place of beauty. Then they spotted food – lots of it!

"You must be starving. Have some supper, please," Suki rattled off as she was already putting a meal out for her guests.

Crocky could not believe his continuing luck. Not only had he escaped from Dan and Stan at the animal park, he had now been invited into a Cornish bakers' kitchen for supper! This was well worth the long, cold and wet journey. Placed in front of Chookoo and Crocky were an array of delicacies: Cornish pasties, sausage rolls, Cornish cream, scones, jam, butter, chocolate cakes, Bakewell tarts... You name it, it seemed to be there.

SNAP, nom, nom, nom, went the ravenous reptile.

Within an instant, all the food that Suki had put out in

front of Crocky and Chookoo had gone inside Crocky's tummy.

"Wow, and I thought I was a fast eater," laughed Suki. "There's plenty more. We have more unsold stock than usual. The weather has stopped people being able to get here. They hope to re-open the main road out of town tomorrow, but this extra rain today has really not helped. Flooding and landslides have closed it in a number of places. They are even having to rebuild it in parts where it's been washed away. But Crocky, please, could you let Chookoo have first refusal on what I bring over next before you start munching again?"

"Of course, *SNAP*. I might beat you for speed of eating, but I have no chance beating you for speed of talking!" replied Crocky with a cheeky glint in his eye.

They all laughed and tucked in. Crocky slowed down his eating speed and decided not to clear out the whole bakery. That would have been unfair to Suki, who was showing him kindness and friendship. They chatted about the escape as they ate. Suki was full of admiration for their achievements.

As they finished eating, Crocky piped up, "I'd better leave first thing tomorrow. They'll discover that I've gone when the morning shift comes on duty in a few hours. Then they will search for me. Also whilst these pastries, cakes and things are really great, thank you, I still need to catch up with all the chocolate I missed from Christmas! What about you, Chookoo?"

Chookoo thought for a few seconds and replied, "I like it here in Cornwall. My family left for a new life in Perthshire, Scotland. They love it up there, but I could not bring myself to leave my Cornish home and friends. So, if you don't mind, Crocky, I think I'll stay and rebuild my home somewhere near here."

"Of course I don't mind, you silly sausage," replied Crocky. "I owe you my freedom, my dear friend. Here, have some walnuts."

Crocky seemed to grab at his skin near his chest area and appeared to start peeling it off. Chookoo and Suki looked open-mouthed in anguished astonishment. Suddenly, much to their relief, they realised that Crocky was in fact wearing a crocodile skin, sleeveless jacket. It was such a good match to his natural colouring that it was virtually impossible to tell what was a jacket and what were his actual scales. Inside his jacket, Crocky had hidden many of the walnuts from the tree in his old enclosure.

"My word, Crocky!" shouted Chookoo, as he rushed to give him a big hug. "That is amazing. You're like a mobile nut store. Thank you so much!"

Suki looked quizzically at Crocky and asked the obvious question, "Where did you get that jacket?"

"Oh," said Crocky. "Before I went to the animal park, I was kept in a farm. My old mate Cecil was a rather large snake there. I watched him shed his whole skin one day and I thought that was rather cool. I asked him if he could teach me his trick. It wasn't very exciting for a lot of the time at that farm so I wanted to do something to alleviate the boredom. Cecil told me to find a loose scale or a ridge on my skin, pull it and see what happened. So that night, after everyone was asleep, I looked at my tummy and saw this slightly raised line that went from the middle of my neck to just above my tail. I pulled it. Amazingly, it all came off like a perfectly fitted jacket. I had brand new scales underneath as well. I couldn't believe it. This jacket has a number of flaps on the inside that work like pockets. It is also brilliantly elasticated so it fits snuggly whether I have my jacket stuffed with things like walnuts or not. The scales at the front of the jacket incredibly re-seal when I put it on, so no one can tell I'm wearing it unless I point it out. Once I made it, I thought this might come in really handy in the future, so I once I put it on, I have never taken it off since."

As Crocky was telling his story, Mary was listening. She was checking on Crocky's progress. Mary allowed herself a smile of satisfaction at how well her jacket-making magic had worked. Whilst Crocky was at the farm, Mary knew that if she could not find any other way to get him out of there, she would have to make sure he escaped. The jacket would keep him warm if he had to flee and it would be a practical place in which Crocky could hide food or other things needed to make any escape a success.

When Crocky finished speaking, everyone in the barn

laughed together before they were interrupted by a loud rumble from Crocky's tummy.

Crocky looked at his stomach and asked, "I don't suppose you have any more pasties, Suki? Pretty please, *SNAP*?"

Suki giggled and handed over another Cornish pasty, which disappeared into Crocky's tummy in a flash.

The three animals then made their way out of the kitchen, across the courtyard and into a barn on the opposite side. Within the barn, they made themselves comfortable for some sleep. Chookoo and Suki curled up amongst some hay bales. Crocky found a large sack of mainly chicken feathers and snuggled right in. They all fell asleep very quickly.

Dawn was barely breaking when Crocky and Chookoo were awoken by an enormous *BANG!* Chookoo shot into the barn's rafters. Crocky ducked his head so he was completely covered by feathers. He soon wished he hadn't because the feathers started to tickle his nose, which set off lots of sneezes.

Suki, though, did not seem at all fazed.

She opened one bleary eye and shouted, "Come in, Ella. It's in the usual place."

In through the barn door came the most glorious creature – but she knew it! Ella was a white-tailed eagle, who lived in the Isle of Wight. She came over to the Trelawny's premises once a month to help herself to some of the finest, only slightly out-of-date, cuts of meat.

Ella was huge. Her beak and talons were as shining and sharp as the finest Sheffield steel knives. Her feathers looked as if they had been prepared and arranged to be worn at Royal Ascot. This was clearly no accident. This was a bird who wanted to make an immediate impression – and she succeeded. She strode confidently over to a large crate in the corner of the barn to her left, grabbed the top of it in her beak, and then nonchalantly threw it to one side. This revealed a number of slightly discoloured cuts of meat, which would have been very expensive to buy a few days earlier when fresh.

Ella squawked in delight, "My darling Suki. You have excelled yourself again. What an absolutely glorious spread. Top drawer!"

Ella spoke with an almost haughty and forced aristocratic tone. It reminded Crocky and Chookoo of the kind of comedy voice they would have expected to hear in a theatrical work as a parody of poshness. They were amazed and for a moment they had to compose themselves against breaking out into giggles.

Chookoo came down from the barn's roof rather tentatively. Crocky popped his head out of his feathery hiding place, announcing his arrival with a loud sneeze.

"Bless you," said Ella. "My dearest Suki, who are these two

fine gentlefolk."

Suki led the introductions and all four started to chat amicably as Ella enjoyed her breakfast. After a few minutes, Suki decided that everyone else needed something to eat too and so she briefly left the barn before returning with a number of Danish pastries.

"Tuck in Crocky and Chookoo," said Suki.

They did not need asking twice.

As they ate and chatted, Crocky had an idea.

"My dear and glorious eagle, Ella. I don't believe I have ever been introduced to such a strong and fine eagle as you in my whole life," said Crocky, trying to flatter her. It succeeded. The terribly vain eagle lapped it up. She stood up even taller, stuck out her chest and her eyes shone even brighter than before. Crocky was not even telling an untruth because he had never been introduced to any eagle before in his life!

Crocky continued, "Would it be possible for you to give me a lift on your way back to the Isle of Wight, please? You see that very soon there are likely to be lots of humans after me and I need to get out of Cornwall as soon as possible."

Suddenly, Chookoo had a brainwave. "Do you know the Beavers in the Otter, Ella?"

Crocky looked at his friend confused.

Beavers in an otter? he thought to himself. *That sounds ridiculous… or painful… or both! Maybe the trials and tribulations of the last few days have finally been too much for Chookoo. He must need a rest.*

Chookoo noticed his friend's bemused look and raised a quizzical eyebrow in his direction. Crocky took that as an invitation to ask his friend what he meant because he did not have a clue.

"How do you get beavers in an otter? Doesn't the otter complain? Doesn't it hurt?" Crocky babbled in a confused fashion.

Chookoo chuckled and replied, "Over in Devon, there's a really beautiful river called the Otter. It is famous, so far as humans are concerned, for its beavers. It is very confusing, but you know what humans can be like."

Everyone nodded in unison.

"So are there no otters in the Otter, then?" asked Crocky.

"Oh yes, there are otters in the Otter, but humans focus on the beavers in the Otter, not the otters in the Otter," said Chookoo, not really helping Crocky's understanding with this explanation.

He saw Crocky's baffled expression and asked, "Dear Ella, you are obviously very well-travelled, I wonder if you could help explain this to Crocky as I feel I'm not doing a very good job."

The grand eagle moved her head slowly from side to side in an exaggerated show of splendour.

She started, "Well, the humans managed to hunt all of the English beavers to extinction. But a few years back, they suddenly came across this beaver family in the Otter just by Easter Bunny Meadow."

"Easter Bunny Meadow?" gasped Crocky. "You mean the real Easter Bunny Meadow?"

Ella carried on, "Oh yes, it's an underground complex where the Easter Bunny's team sort out all of their chocolate for the whole of England. The humans don't have a clue it's there and they will never find it. Magic keeps it hidden from them. They just see a flood plain meadow. But all of us birds and animals know it's there and we can all visit it. It is truly massive. There are always job opportunities there for any non-human creatures but the best time to visit is on Easter Monday. On that day every year, the complex puts on a massive party to celebrate the end of Easter and all the hard work of its staff. It's free and any non-human can join in whether they are a worker or not. The Easter Bunny always ensures that there are loads of free chocolates and other goodies to sample as a thank-you to everybody."

Crocky licked his lips at this information.

"Now where was I about the beavers?" Ella paused for a moment to gather her thoughts. "The humans were shocked to find beavers there. They tried to work it out but they hadn't a clue. But it did encourage them to bring some more beavers to the Otter, so that was good."

"Do you know how the beavers turned up there?" asked Suki, winking at Ella.

"Well, I used to holiday regularly in Bavaria," smiled Ella. "The alps and their foothills are so beautiful and very different to the rolling scenery of the Isle of Wight. I met Bernhard and Steffi there. They are a lovely beaver couple and so welcoming. You haven't tasted Black Forest gateau until you've tasted their special recipe. They borrowed it from some humans and improved it!"

"Yum, yum, *SNAP*," interjected Crocky.

"Yum, yum indeed, my dear crocodile. But one year I turned up and they were in turmoil. Their wonderful home had just been smashed by a new Autobahn, I mean motorway, bridge. They were distraught and could not bring themselves to move elsewhere in Bavaria. You see, nothing there could be as good as their old home, they thought. They could not stand watching what the humans were doing. So I offered them a way out and a new beginning."

Ella continued, "The Otter is a perfect place for beavers. Even the humans protect large sections of the river from destruction and pollution. It has lovely trout, which a nicely placed dam could help to catch. Then any adorable, friendly and hungry eagle, who might just happen to be passing, could pop in and offer to take any surplus trout off their paws – just to reduce wastage, of course!"

Everyone chuckled at that comment.

"But seriously, darlings, I chatted with Bernhard and Steffi about this divine location for many hours. I also might have suggested that it could be rather beneficial to a lovely pair of beavers, who had perfected the art of making Black Forest gateau, to move to Devon. After all, the UK has a huge tradition in chocolate making and artistry, and Devon, just like its neighbour Cornwall, is renowned for the most delicious cream, dairy and bakery ingredients and creations. It was a very hard decision for them but they agreed that my suggestions made a lot of sense, packed their belongings and I flew them over. They've never looked back. Six youngsters proves it!" laughed Ella, with all of the others joining in.

"I'm glad you remembered Cornwall is also famous for its cream, diary and bakery products," said Suki.

Ella giggled. "I wouldn't dream of forgetting that when I'm in a Cornish bakery!"

Ella finished her story, "And, my darlings, to this day the humans still have no idea how beavers returned to England!"

She then started to preen herself in delight and self-congratulation.

Crocky's brain had gone into overdrive as he listened to all of this. He needed a safe place to hide away. It needed to be away from East Cornwall. In the neighbouring county, there was a secret chocolate complex, which was open to recruiting new animal staff, and a friendly beaver family, who had a fantastic Black Forest gateau recipe. This was the perfect place for Crocky. The ever-watchful Mary agreed.

Crocky coughed slightly to gain the eagle's attention, "My divine Ella, I'd love to see your good friends and I reckon I could help them deal with all of these floods that they must also be suffering. Too much water plays havoc with dams and rivers. We crocodiles are quite strong and not bad swimmers, you know, so I'm sure that I could assist over there. It would also get me safely away from East Cornwall until everything quietens down and I can decide where I would like to settle for the longer term."

Crocky paused and looked at Ella, whom he could see was pondering what he was saying.

He then moved into full-on flattery mode, "I hope you don't mind me asking but isn't Devon on the way to the Isle of Wight? Whilst I could try walking to the River Otter, I fear I would be spotted and re-captured rather quickly. Would it be possible for you to give me a lift by flying me over there whenever you return home, please? If truth be told, I have an ulterior motive. I hope I'm not being a bit too forward but I would also love to see close up the poetic grace of your flying."

Crocky wondered if he had gone too far with this final comment. He needn't have worried. Ella lapped it up.

"My dear Crocky. You're so welcome and so right about my flying," fluttered Ella. "Come on, come on. There's no time to waste. The weather is set fair for the next few hours – although the north-easterly wind is bitter. You'd better wrap up!"

Crocky jumped up. He ran to the sack of feathers and stuffed his jacket full of them for insulation. When he turned around, he noticed that his three friends were already outside the barn in the courtyard. Crocky joined them. He walked over to Suki and gave her a big hug of thanks as he said goodbye to her.

Then he turned to Chookoo. They looked at each other and a few tears started to well up in their eyes. They gave each other a long, emotional and heartfelt embrace before wishing each other the best of luck with their new adventures.

Almost as soon as Crocky and Chookoo disengaged, Crocky felt himself being lifted up very quickly by two enormous taloned feet. He looked up and saw the most magnificent eight-feet-wide wingspan, which was taking him into the morning sky. Now he really felt free!

The journey to the River Otter in the crisp spring air was beautiful but every bit as freezing as Ella had warned. Crocky could feel every part of his body not covered by his jacket going numb with the cold. Even his body, encased in the feather-padded jacket, was not exactly toasty to say the least. Crocky tried to looked on the positive side that he would have been even colder without it and his chilly discomfort was a minor price to pay to complete his escape. This only partly worked.

The journey acquainted Crocky with Ella's passion. When she flew, she loved to sing – very loudly. What was more, Ella thought she was a brilliant singer. She did not even consider the possibility that not everyone might share her opinion of her musical prowess. In fact, she was an awful singer, who had little knowledge of the real words to any song, but no one had ever had the heart or bravery to tell her.

In between songs, Ella explained to Crocky that she had a wide taste in music. Her favourite song was a French-language one called, "Ella, elle l'a." Ella did not understand French. She thought the song was called, "Ella, Ella" and it just kept repeating her name with lots of "doo, doo, doo, doo" sounds. She genuinely believed that the song was named after her as she flew over France to Bavaria. Mary's magic meant Crocky did understand French and he had heard a version of the real song over the radio when at the farm. Whilst he knew it had absolutely nothing to do with Ella Eagle, or any other eagles for that matter, he formed the view that it would not help him to point that out. Ella loved her interpretation of this song so much, she kept singing it. In fact, after every third or fourth other song had emanated harshly from her beak, she would squawk this one out again and again.

This meant that Crocky spent the whole journey with a Hobson's choice. He could either use the feathers from his jacket and stuff them in his ears trying to shut out Ella's appallingly, dreadful and repetitive singing but completely freeze, or he could keep a bit warmer with the feathers remaining where he had stuffed them whilst his eardrums were hammered. With a very heavy heart, Crocky chose the latter. When Ella finally landed and deposited Crocky at the Beaver household, Crocky was beyond relieved that the assault upon his ears had come to an end.

When Crocky and Ella arrived, Gerhard, Steffi and their six children were busy repairing their nearby dam. They had constructed it a few years previously, but it had been damaged by all the incessant rain and flood water, just as Crocky had thought. An old orange traffic cone had been swept downstream and the tip of it was stuck fast in the middle of the dam.

The eldest Beaver child, called Anton, came over nervously with a large trout in his mouth. He dropped it before Ella and said, "Please, ma'am, please accept our gift to you for your help and friendship."

Ella was ecstatic with this welcome. Being handed a big fresh fish and being referred to in a similar manner as Her Majesty the Queen re-affirmed her not-so-modest view that she had posh, powerful and almost regal poise and personality. She fluffed up her feathers, stretched her neck as high as it would go and beamed at Anton.

Ella spoke to the young beaver with an almost triumphant air, "Thank you, Master Anton. That looks delicious. My word, you are a fine young man and a credit to your parents. I see that you and all of your brothers and sisters look so much bigger than the last time I saw you."

Anton looked at his feet, embarrassed. He was a shy but well-brought-up young beaver. He had been asked by his parents to give Ella this trout as a present. It was one of those parental requests that a child would really prefer not to do, but he knew it was actually an order rather than an ask. It was bad enough being obliged to do this when he was painfully socially awkward, but it was made many times worse because he had no idea how to address an important family friend and visitor. He had a vague memory from playing kings and queens games as a younger child about how to address royalty, but that was all. The way he had addressed Ella was all he could think of in his fear at being thrust into this social situation for which he felt he had no aptitude. Hence, Ella received this greeting as if she were royalty by pure accident of circumstances. But she loved it!

Ella bent forward and picked up the trout in her beak. Three bites later and it was gone. By this time, Bernhard and Steffi had joined the small group. After Ella had thanked them for the fish, she introduced Crocky to them and they chatted about his predicament. Crocky liked Bernhard and Steffi. They were friendly, caring and lovely animals.

After about twenty minutes of chatting and laughing, Ella looked into the sky, paused for a couple of seconds and stated, "Looks like the wind direction is changing and I don't fancy flying back across the Solent into a headwind. I must dash off home now. See you all again soon. I know the Beavers will look after you, Crocky, until you find somewhere else to settle. Farewell!"

And with a flamboyant spin and flourish of her wings, Ella took to the sky. She flew off very quickly in the direction of the Isle of Wight.

Steffi looked at Crocky and said, "Come in. You must be cold and starving. Do you like gateau? When we were living in Bavaria, we weren't that far from the Black Forest, and we learnt about a really good cake recipe. I hope you like it?"

"*SNAP!* Oh yes! *SNAP!* I love all gateaux! But I particularly love Black Forest gateau!" cried Crocky joyously. Everyone laughed. Crocky all but skipped behind the Beaver family into their home and prepared to tuck in.

Chapter Eleven

Call the Police

Whilst Crocky was making good his escape from Cornwall, the morning shift arrived for work at the animal park. Two of those staff members were Jen and Ken. They were good, experienced professionals, who loved their jobs and loved animals even more. They were tasked with opening up and checking the whole of the building containing the crocodile enclosure.

When they walked up to the building's main doors, everything looked just like a normal day. They opened them, moved inside and switched off the alarms. They went over to the key cabinet and removed the keys to Crocky's old living area. They glanced at Crocky's pond and saw what they thought was Crocky lying in his normal position in the pond.

Jen and Ken made their way back outside the building and put one of the keys into the crocodile enclosure's outside door. To their surprise, they found it was unlocked. They were a little concerned about this, but no more than that. They opened that door and entered the holding area. In a half-joking manner, Jen decided to try the handle to the enclosure's inside door without bothering with a key. It opened immediately. By now, Jen and Ken were becoming very anxious.

They stepped purposefully into the enclosure. They walked up to the pond to check on Crocky. He had gone. All that was in Crocky's usual place was a two-feet-long branch with a bit of crocodile skin on it.

Jen gasped. "My word, our crocodile's gone! Oh no! They've left some of his scales on that bit of wood. That's despicable. They haven't just stolen him. They've skinned him – in his own home too!"

Mary was not expecting any humans to think that Crocky had been stolen for his skin. The scales on the log were just meant to act as a type of decoy. Nevertheless, Mary considered that this turn of events could be useful.

Ken's reaction to Crocky's disappearance was at first muted. He stood staring at the branch in open-mouthed disbelief, trying to process what had happened in his mind. After about a minute, his brain had worked it out and agreed with Jen's hypothesis. Then Ken burst into tears. That set off Jen.

Shaking with emotion, Jen took out her mobile phone and called the park owners. Sam and Nik were working on the other side of the site. When the answered her call, all the owners could hear was indecipherable sobbing. They stopped what they were doing and ran over to see what had caused such upset. When they found out, floods of tears cascaded out of their eyes too.

Sam and Nik were pillars of East Cornish society. They were also very good friends with the area's chief constable.

They had met each other on a number of occasions at various local charity events. The chief constable took a keen interest in conservation and animal welfare. She was also the English Police Forces' national lead for rural crime and ending animal abuse.

At one charity function, the chief constable had been so impressed by the conservation and animal welfare work being done by Sam and Nik that she gave them her personal direct phone number should any animal emergency arise. Hitherto, there had been no reason to use it as this part of Cornwall was usually extremely law-abiding. Now there was.

The imaginations of Sam and Nik were running wild. They thought of their missing crocodile. They had seen remnants of his skin lying on a branch, which had been left in his favourite spot. Like Jen and Ken, they came to the horrible conclusion that Crocky had been stolen for his skin. Suddenly, it dawned upon them that their animal park must have been targeted by illegal animal skin traders, who were very likely to come back for their other animals. These fears convinced them that they had to call the Chief Constable of East Cornwall on her direct line immediately.

Sam just beat Nik to make the phone call. The chief constable answered within two rings. She was shocked. She re-assured Sam that she would get her best officers on the case at once.

True to her word, the chief constable even emailed her

top detective team as Sam was still speaking with her. As soon as their call ended, the chief constable followed up her email and phoned Detective Inspector Liz MacEwan.

DI MacEwan had been with East Cornwall Constabulary since she was eighteen years old. She was Cornish-born- and bred. She had an intricate knowledge of, and cared deeply for, the whole area and its people. Her skill and intelligence had led to numerous promotions. She was admired by all colleagues at every level as an extremely talented and tenacious detective and leader. She listened intently to her chief constable. She knew whom she wanted to assign to help her with this most important job. The top detective sergeant and top detective constable in East Cornwall were under her command. They were Detective Sergeant Asif Iqbal and Detective Constable Yash Kohli.

DS Iqbal and DC Kohli were keen. They loved their jobs. They had huge experience. They were fast. They were efficient. They always worked together. Their case-solving rate was the best in England. And they thought they were comedians.

DS Iqbal and DC Kohli were both in long-term relationships. They were also fathers of teenage children. They had developed their comedic skills over many years. Opinion was divided about the quality of their humour within their households; albeit not equally. They thought that they were good enough to earn money on the stand-up circuit. Their families believed that their abilities plumbed new depths of what their children called, "Dreadful Dad Jokes."

It was after dinner on an icy Boxing Day a few years previously when DS Iqbal's partner reached the end of her tether with his funny act at home. For the first time in years, DS Iqbal had been at home from Christmas Eve through to the Feast of Stephen. This meant that his whole family had been subjected to nearly three whole days of incessantly awful jokes. In exasperation, his partner suggested that he needed to take his routine to a new arena because his 'professional' standard of entertainment was too intricate and too niche for his family to understand or appreciate. DS Iqbal's one failing, like that of his colleague DC Kohli, was an inability to acknowledge the limitations of his comic ability. Due to this, he did not spot the sarcasm of his partner's comments.

DS Iqbal considered what his partner had said overnight and agreed with the sentiments. When he returned to work the next day, he discussed those comments with DC Kohli. His close colleague concurred that his family did not seem to be able to appreciate fully his comedic output either. The two detectives decided that henceforth, they would concentrate their main humorous efforts away from their families. They decided to expand their performances and turn them into practical skills, which they could use as part of their interviewing techniques when questioning suspects.

When they returned to their homes later that day, they told their families what they had agreed to do. Their loved ones did not know whether to laugh or cry, or even if these detectives were being serious. They soon discovered that not only did they really mean it, but they had started to do it. Their households found that the number of terrible jokes they had to endure reduced markedly because DS Iqbal and DC Kohli were quite happy to showcase the vast majority of their humour at work. On occasions, their families did briefly reflect upon how the hapless suspects of East Cornwall were finding these new unique interrogation methods. They would then count their blessings. Indeed, DC Kohli's family felt forever grateful to DS Iqbal's partner for the idea!

As soon as DI MacEwan finished her chat with her chief constable, she contacted DS Iqbal and DC Kohli about their new investigation. She knew that as soon as she started briefing them, they would already be working on lines of enquiry and emailing lots of people within the police service for assistance. She was correct.

DI MacEwan had some extremely urgent other work to complete before she could give her full and undivided attention to the Crocky investigation. This meant it was about two hours later before DI MacEwan drove into the car park of the animal park. As she alighted from her police vehicle, she found the crime scene swarming with police, forensic scientists, scene of crime investigators and a range of other experts in numerous technological and other fields.

As she was walking away from her car, her mobile phone buzzed with a message. It was from DS Iqbal.

"Two suspects identified. Uniformed colleagues on way to

arrest!"

DI MacEwan smiled at the screen.

She messaged back, *"Well done! Meet me in the car park in my car for a debrief in 5! Bring DC Kohli."*

She returned to her car, opened it again and sat in the driver's seat. In exactly five minutes, DS Iqbal and DC Kohli joined her, grinning broadly. They were excited and proud to be doing such an important and interesting job. In all of their years of service, they had never dealt with an illegal animal skin trading case before. They were having fun.

Whilst the three detectives were debriefing and brainstorming in DI MacEwan's car, four uniformed police constables were knocking very loudly upon the front door of an apartment about ten miles away. This was the home of Dan and Stan, where they lived together as flatmates. Even though it was late morning for many, for Dan and Stan it was still very much slumber time. They did not appreciate the noisy and abrupt way they had been woken up. They were even more unhappy when they opened the door and found themselves being arrested for burglary, theft and illegal animal skin trading relating to Crocky's disappearance. The police then gave the sleepy-eyed Dan and Stan some personal time, in which to wake up fully, in the back of a police van as they were driven to East Cornwall Constabulary's Headquarters for questioning.

Mary Mermicorn was paying close attention to all of this.

She could not believe how the humans had misinterpreted this straightforward 'skin on log' trick.

As Mary considered this human investigative error, she recalled these words of her old principal at the Mermicorn Magic College, "Humans get many things right, but they also get many things wrong. Mermicorns can only do our duties. On occasions, our duties might give humans some information. Unless our duties demand otherwise, what humans do with that information, whether right or wrong, is their business alone. Mermicorns have no role in correcting human mistakes!"

The three detectives were still in DI MacEwan's car when DC Kohli's phone rang with news of the arrests. He passed on this information to his two colleagues immediately. They all paused for a moment and smiled to themselves. DI MacEwan then wrapped up their conversation. She asked DS Iqbal and DC Kohli to return to their police headquarters as soon as possible to interview Dan and Stan. DI MacEwan told them that she would stay at the animal park to continue directing the investigations there. She said that she would ensure that they were kept up-to-date with all important developments.

DS Iqbal and DC Kohli smiled even more at this request. They really liked interviewing suspects. They thanked their inspector and bid her goodbye. They left her vehicle and almost bounced along to their police car in their eagerness to get back to their headquarters for the interviews. They jumped into their transport and drove off.

The interview style of DS Iqbal and DC Kohli was legendary throughout East Cornwall. They did not go in for using naughty language, shouting or raised voices. Their skill was in finding holes in suspects' stories and highlighting them very vividly. They were brilliant at interviewing not only due to their high levels of intelligence and natural talent, but also because they prepared all of their interviews together and extremely thoroughly.

As much as they loved interviewing people, the feeling was certainly not shared by their interviewees or their lawyers. Most suspects thought that DS Iqbal and DC Kohli enjoyed their jobs far too much and should try something else.

DS Iqbal and DC Kohli arrived at the headquarters with their usual positive and confident manner. They had been in this type of situation on many previous occasions. They knew exactly what was expected of them and they disappeared into the building to ensure that they delivered.

Chapter Twelve

Mary's Investigative Interventions

Mary Mermicorn hated bullies. Dan and Stan were bullies. She wondered if their appalling behaviour had only started when they began working at the animal park or if it was a more long-term thing. She decided to find out. Mermicorns can travel back in time but not into the future. She decided to go back in time and see what Dan and Stan were really like. The answer was not at all good.

She discovered that Dan and Stan met in secondary school. They became inseparable friends from the beginning. Unfortunately, their friendship was based upon being horrible. Their main forms of enjoyment involved bullying, thieving, selfishness, and other forms of unpleasantness towards humans and animals alike. In spite of this, they had never been caught by the police or by any other officialdom. A mixture of scaring people into silence or making sure that there was no evidence of their bad behaviour had made sure of this. Mary soon realised that they never thought they would ever get caught, they had no intention of changing their behaviour, they only cared about themselves and they enjoyed being bad.

However, it was their behaviour at every location where they had worked together – and there were three of them, which completely astounded her. She had assumed that they had only started stealing together at the animal park: how wrong did she turn out to be!

After Dan and Stan left secondary school, they spent two unproductive years at college before entering the labour market. At first, they worked for different employers. None of their jobs lasted very long. They always ended up getting the sack for some rule-breaking. That all changed about a year ago, when they decided that they would work together and have some 'fun'.

They managed to get jobs with West Tamar Valley Hospital Cleaners. They were on the early evening shift. Their jobs were to clean a number of public areas, which included a snack bar with its own kitchen. That bar had closed by the time they started their shifts. Its kitchen was locked and alarmed just like the one at the animal park. The entrance to that kitchen was covered by a CCTV camera. In that kitchen, food and drink was stored, ready-prepared for sale to the public over the next day or so. Dan and Stan worked out where the kitchen keys were kept and how to turn the CCTV and alarm systems on and off. So it was at this hospital where they started their careers as kitchen burglars, stealing food and drink. As long as they did not take too much, no one seemed to notice.

After a few months working at the hospital, they thought that they had better move on in case someone eventually realised what they were doing. They managed to get very similar jobs, again with early evening shifts, working for West Tamar Valley Council's Cleaning Services. They ensured that they worked near to a public snack bar, which had closed by the time their shifts started. Of course, this snack bar had its own kitchen, which was stocked with food and drink ready for the next day or so. Once there, just like they had done at the hospital, they worked out how to get the kitchen keys, how to turn the CCTV and alarm systems on and off, and they carried on their careers as kitchen burglars.

Dan and Stan followed the same plan that had been so successful at the hospital. After a few months working at the council, they decided to move jobs to reduce the risk of getting caught. Ironically, by this time they had good references from both the hospital and the council, which enabled them to get very similar early evening jobs with the animal park.

They had only intended to work and burgle the kitchen there for a few months before moving to another unsuspecting employer. The only real difference between their work at the animal park and their two previous jobs was that they had to work with Crocky. This gave them the chance to show another highly unpleasant part of their personalities, which was illustrated by how they spoke to him and treated him.

Mary had her magic duty to provide Crocky with unique protections against humanity. So far as she was concerned, the concept of humanity could mean any number of people between one human to the whole human race. This meant she could use the spell to do a very wide range of things to protect Crocky from Dan and Stan. Mary knew that they had just been arrested for crimes that they had not committed. She thought that it would only be a matter of time before the police worked out that they were innocent and let them go. When that happened, Mary knew that they would go back to work at the animal park, where they would just continue their dreadful behaviour. Mary also understood that she could not guarantee that Crocky would never be found and returned to the animal park. If that happened, Crocky would be subjected to continuing unpleasantness by Dan and Stan once again.

Mary could not risk this possibility and stay true to the spell's intentions. Mary decided that she had to interpret the spell to do something to stop Dan and Stan from ever being able to look after or be nasty to Crocky again. She knew that the only way to do this was to stop Dan and Stan working at the animal park. Mary had one problem with this idea. However much she tried, she could not work out how to do it.

As Mary pondered this conundrum, she was watching the police investigations. She heard DI MacEwan being asked to look at the animal park's CCTV footage and alarm activation records. This was causing the police a great deal of interest. The police had found evidence that Dan and Stan had turned the CCTV and alarms off for about a quarter of an hour during their shift on the evening before Crocky was discovered missing.

The police then checked the previous day's CCTV footage and alarm activation records. The same thing happened at almost exactly the same time for about a quarter of an hour. Intrigued by this potential pattern, the police kept checking the CCTV footage and alarm activation records during every day Dan and Stan worked at the animal park. The same thing happened every single day since they started working there, but it did not happen at all before they joined.

DI MacEwan was intrigued. She wondered what other criminality they were doing. She knew that the kitchen was the only area in the building that had been alarmed before Dan and Stan started their shift. She had also ascertained that those alarms were always deactivated and reactivated whilst they were at work.

DI MacEwan went to see the kitchen staff, who were waiting patiently in another part of the animal park, to see if they could provide any useful additional information. She asked them to check if anything was missing from the kitchen. Within a few minutes, they started to discover that stock was missing. Further checks indicated that food and drink must have been stolen over a number of days. The kitchen staff began a full stock-take covering the whole period when Dan and Stan worked at the animal park and the month beforehand. The full picture of their stealing at the animal park was soon uncovered.

Mary watched this impressive police work and had a brainwave. Now the police were getting on the right track about what crimes Dan and Stan had actually done, she wanted to make sure that they were caught for their stealing from their last two jobs as well. Mary believed that they might not get much of a punishment for stealing food and drink from one place of work, and that would mean that they would have a chance of keeping their jobs and causing Crocky great harm and distress should he be recaptured. However, if she could assist the police to discover that Dan and Stan had been stealing from all three places where they worked together, Mary knew enough about how humans treated their criminals to be quite certain that in those circumstances she could completely protect Crocky from Dan and Stan because they would get prison sentences and lose their jobs with the animal park.

Mary hurriedly checked the CCTV footage and alarm records for the local hospital and local council. To her dismay, she discovered that all of the potential evidence of Dan and Stan's thieving had been lost because those systems only retained that information for a month. As she threw her head back and shook her mane in frustration, she was struck with a second brainwave. Mary paused to contemplate if this would work. Suddenly, she threw her head back again but this time she was whinnying to the heavens in glee.

Her solution was inspired. It followed on from her vivid recollection of her discussions with the mermaid queen. She knew that the Mermaid and Mermicorn Royal Rules allowed her to go into the past but with big restrictions about what she was allowed to do there. Whilst these rules banned her from making her presence known to anyone in the past, and they prohibited her from communicating and interacting with any creatures or beings in the past, these rules were created many years before things like CCTV or electronic alarm systems were even pipedreams, let alone a reality. Mary's eureka moment came when she recognised what was obvious: CCTV and alarm systems were neither creatures nor beings so the rules did not stop her going into the past and interfering with them.

As soon as Mary spotted this, her plans to protect Crocky quickly fell into place. These rules did not stop her from going into the past and casting a spell to change the retention periods of the CCTV footage and alarm records at the hospital and the council from one month to two years. This would allow the police to get the necessary evidence from the CCTV and alarm systems at those premises to prove that Dan and Stan has been stealing from there as well. Mary was not going to change how anyone behaved in the past. She was not going to cause new records to be made. All she was going to do was make sure that all records that were made were available to the police investigators. This was not going to stop any other recordings from happening, change anything else, or involve any interactions with any creatures or beings in the past. So Mary reckoned that what she was going to do was completely legal under the rules.

Mary took a deep breath. She had never gone back in time before to cast a spell. She remembered being taught at the Mermicorn Magic College that if she ever tried to pass an unlawful spell, not only it would it not be allowed but she would then be recalled immediately to the Mermicorn Palace to face disciplinary action. Any mermicorn found to have tried to pass an illegal spell could expect to be removed forthwith from the list of trained mermicorns, who were allowed to carry out mermaid spells. Whilst Mary was sure that what she planned to do was lawful, the fact that she had never done anything like this before and the consequences to her career of getting it wrong started to play on her mind and cause her to doubt herself.

After a few minutes of anxious consideration, Mary's thoughts came to the conclusion, "I have to do this for the sake of Crocky and so many others."

She took a deep breath and sent herself back in time by eighteen months. She wanted to get her magic done as quickly as possible because she feared that the longer she was in the past, the greater the chance that she would mess up. As soon as she arrived eighteen months in the past, Mary closed her eyes and with great concentration she cast a spell to extend the retention periods of the hospital and council CCTV and alarm systems to two years. As soon as she finished that magic, she returned to the present. In all, it took less than a minute, but to Mary it felt a lot longer.

Mary stood like a statue with her eyes closed fearing the worst, but nothing happened to her. She opened her eyes very slowly, half-expecting a royal mermicorn guard to be there telling her that her spell was not allowed and summoning her to the king's palace at once. No one seemed to be there. She looked all around her and she was still alone. She smiled weakly to herself, and exhaled loudly in relief. Now she just had to see if the police lines of enquiry would lead them to go to the hospital and council to check these retained records. Mary did not have to wait very long.

As soon as DI MacEwan became aware of the evidence suggesting that Dan and Stan had been continually burgling the kitchen near Crocky's enclosure, she wanted to see if they had done anything similar in their previous jobs. She sent a number of police officers to do these checks. East Cornwall Constabulary was very pleasantly surprised to find all of the CCTV and alarm evidence still in existence at the hospital and the council. That led to rapid stock-taking exercises. In very quick time, Dan and Stan's burgling course of conduct at those other workplaces was revealed in full.

Chapter Thirteen

Interview Time

Whilst Mary was helping the police to obtain key evidence, DS Iqbal and DC Kohli had finished their interview planning. They decided that DS Iqbal would be the main interrogator, whilst DC Kohli provided the supporting act. The only thing upon which they could not decide was whom they would interview first. After much debating, DC Kohli fished out an old dirty penny coin, which he kept in his jacket for these situations. He showed it to DS Iqbal, who knew exactly what he meant and smirked at his partner.

"Heads it's Dan, tails it's Stan," called DS Iqbal, as DC Kohli tossed the penny into the air.

The coin landed onto the tiled floor of the police station with a tinny clatter.

"It's heads!" they called in unison. "Let's give Dan the good news!"

Dan and his lawyer were then invited into the interview room.

After all of the introductions, and a few gentle starter questions, which were deliberately designed to lull Dan into a false sense of security whilst still elucidating a number of useful admissions from him, DS Iqbal started to get right to business.

"So you have no idea how the crocodile went missing?" asked DS Iqbal.

"No idea at all," replied Dan.

"And you say you've done nothing wrong?" continued DS Iqbal.

"That's right. Nothing wrong at all," stated Dan.

"That's interesting," pondered DS Iqbal, as a large mischievous grin spread over his face. "Watch this CCTV. Could you do the honours please, DC Kohli?"

"Oh course," said DC Kohli, quite merrily.

DC Kohli played the CCTV of the previous evening. Everyone sat and watched.

As the footage played, DS Iqbal started to give a commentary to help Dan, "We see Stan and you are the only people in that building and you both remained the only two persons in that building throughout the whole evening whilst you were there. Do you agree?"

"Yes," mumbled Dan.

DS Iqbal had the key admission he needed from Dan and

he carried on to cement his advantage, "The CCTV shows you two getting the keys to the crocodile enclosure from the key cabinet. We see you going outside, out of the view of the CCTV camera. We know that you two then used those keys to get through the locked outer and inner doors into the enclosure because... there we have it... we now see you two coming into the enclosure through the inner door with the keys in your hands."

"Yeah, and your point is what?" said Dan almost morosely.

"All will come clear soon," said DS Iqbal helpfully. "We now see you both working in the enclosure. We see you both leaving the enclosure, closing the inner door, disappearing out of view again until... here you both come again. We see you entering the main building again. So you locked both the inner and outer doors, didn't you?"

"Of course, we did. We're professionals," stated Dan indignantly.

"I'm pleased to hear it," said DS Iqbal brightly. "Do you also agree that throughout all of this CCTV footage, the crocodile does not move from his spot at all?"

"Of course, he's the laziest animal I've ever come across. I've never seen him move," chuckled Dan, giving a glimpse of his disdain for Crocky.

DS Iqbal noticed this change of mood within Dan. It

pleased him because it indicated that he was becoming a bit more comfortable in the interview. Comfortable criminals can sometimes let their guard down and be tripped up by skilful detectives.

DS Iqbal continued, "If you look about five or six feet up the walnut tree in his enclosure, you can see a small branch that looks about two feet long. It seems a bit wobbly, as if it's not very well attached to the trunk, but at this stage it is still part of that tree."

DC Khohli moved towards the monitor screen and pointed to the branch on the walnut tree that Chookoo later chewed off.

"Thank you, DC Kohli, for pointing it out," said DS Iqbal politely.

"Yes, the CCTV does show all of that. It just shows us doing our jobs. You have no case. Let me go!" exclaimed Dan in defiant exasperation.

"Let's just finish here first," smiled DC Kohli.

DS Iqbal went on, "Stan and you are seen at 19.00 coming into the dining area and putting the doors' keys onto a table there. Look those keys are not being put back into the key cabinet. Why is that?"

Dan stayed silent.

"Then at 19.01, Stan and you walk over to the power switch for this CCTV camera and amazingly... there you go... the camera goes off. Why is that?" asked DC Kohli as he paused the CCTV footage.

Dan gulped but did not answer.

DS Iqbal put a piece of paper onto the table in front of Dan and his solicitor.

DS Iqbal explained, "The piece of paper in front of you is a copy of exhibit TPC/1, which is a print-out of the alarm activations and de-activations for that building for that date. You can see the time the alarms were switched on and off clearly there. Please take your time, Dan, to study that."

Dan and his lawyer studied exhibit TPC/1. Dan coughed; beads of sweat were now starting to form upon his forehead.

DS Iqbal moved on, "We have statements from the kitchen staff and the park owners, who provide clear evidence that the kitchen was locked and its alarm turned on before you and Stan came into that building on the evening in question. Earlier CCTV footage and TPC/1 show that as well. The park owners also say that as soon as the inner and outer doors to the crocodile enclosure are both locked at any time after 18.00, the alarm goes on for that enclosure automatically. You can see on the print-out that happened at 18.59, which is when the CCTV footage shows you both leaving that area. TPC/1 shows that at 19.02, just one minute after the CCTV footage shows Stan and you turning off the CCTV system, the alarms for the enclosure and the kitchen are turned off. Finally TPC/1 shows that none of the alarms were then turned on again until the alarms of the whole building were turned on at 19.16."

DS Iqbal paused for a few seconds to let this sink into Dan's brain.

"Please start the CCTV again, DC Kohli?" asked DS Iqbal.

DC Kohli leant over and started playing the remaining footage.

DS Iqbal carried on, "We see at 19.15, the CCTV is turned on again. It is Stan and you whom we see at the CCTV power switch when this happens. We then see you both pick up the keys from the table, put the keys into the key cabinet, set the alarms at 19.16 (just as the alarm print-out TPC/1 indicates), turn off the lights and leave. As you leave, you both appear to be having quite a jolly laugh. Anything to say about this?"

There was a defending silence from Dan.

DC Kohli paused the CCTV footage. He put two still photographs that had been taken from the CCTV footage in front of Dan and his lawyer.

DS Iqbal grinned and said, "Thank you, DC Khohli. These photos are exhibits ADJ/1 and ADJ/2. Please take your time considering them, Dan. You see ADJ/1 is taken from the CCTV footage. It shows the exact position of the crocodile enclosure's keys just after you both dropped them on the table before you turned off the CCTV system. You see ADJ/2 is also taken from the CCTV footage. That shows the exact position of those keys on that same table just after you turned on the CCTV system, but before you picked them up to put them in the cabinet. Now please look really carefully and compare the two positions. You can see those positions are quite similar but they are clearly different. So at some time, whilst you two had turned off the CCTV system, the keys to the crocodile's enclosure were moved. How did that happen? Why did that happen?"

More silence came from Dan.

DS Iqbal started to ram home his advantage, "Of course, you have earlier agreed that only Stan and you were in this building throughout all of this time. This is supported by the CCTV footage because it does not show anyone else there."

Dan was turning very pale and started to shake his head. He could see the keys had been moved but he had no idea who had moved them or why.

Dan muttered in desperation, "I don't know anything about the keys moving. I can't explain it."

DS Iqbal went on, "The alarms and the CCTV worked perfectly well, except when Stan and you turned them off, all evening and all night between the times when you both arrived for your shift and when the morning shift came on duty. There were no alarm activations or any indications that the alarms or CCTV systems failed during this period or at all. Nobody else is seen on the CCTV until the morning shift turns up. The CCTV shows them coming into the building, switching on the building's lights, turning off the alarms, taking the keys out of the cabinet, leaving the building, and then coming back into view of the CCTV camera as they come through the inner door into the crocodile's enclosure. We know that the two people on the morning shift found the outer and inner doors to the enclosure were unlocked. The CCTV footage then shows the morning shift workers discover that what they thought was the crocodile was in fact a log, lying in the exact spot where the crocodile used to be."

DC Kohli then turned on the CCTV footage once more. He found a clear view of the walnut tree as the morning shift discovered that Crocky was missing. He paused that picture on the screen. He took his pen and used the point of it to indicate the exact position on the walnut tree where the previously seen branch was now missing.

DS Iqbal was in full flow, "Thank you, DC Kohli. We can clearly see that is the position where there had been a branch about two feet long attached to this tree. That attached branch was clearly visible on the previous evening's CCTV footage, which we have shown you already. The branch was there before you and Stan turned off the CCTV for fourteen minutes. Our forensic team has proved that the log, which was found where the crocodile would usually lie, had some crocodile skin on it. Our forensic team has also found out that this log was actually a branch from a walnut tree. That branch is about two feet long, which is almost exactly the same length as the missing crocodile. Our forensic team has worked out that when that branch came off the tree, the end of it which was originally attached to the tree left a slight stub on the tree's trunk. Did you know that this stub works like a jigsaw piece?"

More silence came from Dan.

"Well, our forensic team had found an exact mechanical, jigsaw type fit between the end of the branch that used to be fixed to the tree and the stub it left on that tree's trunk. So we know that the branch, which was left where the crocodile used to lie, which had crocodile skin on it, came from the tree in the crocodile's enclosure. Doesn't all of this evidence prove that the crocodile had his skin removed from him in his enclosure by Stan and you? That explains why we found the skin on the log, doesn't it? The crocodile would not have let you do this without a fight, so a two-feet-long wooden branch would have been very useful to hit and stun him before you took off his skin and stole his body, eh? Then you two placed the log exactly where the crocodile used to lie to make it look like he was still there, didn't you? Anything to say?"

Both detectives looked directly at Dan. They were grinning widely.

Dan did not share their happiness. He was sweating

profusely with liquid dripping down his face and back.

All he could splutter in reply was, "No. I've done nothing."

At that moment, DS Iqbal and DC Kohli decided it was time for a comfort break. Dan and his lawyer weren't going to complain.

During that break, DI MacEwan spoke with DS Iqbal and DC Kohli. She had returned to East Cornwall Constabulary's Headquarters to update them about the current state of the investigation. They came up with what they thought was a really jolly way to introduce the new evidence into the second stage of Dan's interview. They ended their chat in very good spirits. DS Iqbal and DC Kohli finished their cups of tea and went off to start interviewing again.

Chapter Fourteen

The Comedy Duo

DS Iqbal and DC Kohli were very pleased with the first part of the interview but, in spite of the evidence, Dan had not budged from his denials of any criminality. A new tactic was required. They decided to go for their favourite and infamous interview style: the comic duo. They just had to get the interview to the right moment. They agreed that they were nearly there.

DS Iqbal began the next part of Dan's interview smiling even more broadly than he had ended the first part. Dan's lawyer, who knew all about the comic duo, noticed this and waited for the worst for her client.

DS Iqbal started, "OK. What we've found out is that every evening since you two started working at the animal park, the CCTV and alarm systems were turned off at around 19.00, and they were turned on again at about 19.15. So, it was not just the evening when the crocodile vanished that this happened. Our colleagues are now going through all of the CCTV recordings as we speak. What they've viewed so far shows that Stan and you were always responsible for this. So what were you both doing whilst you had turned off the CCTV and alarm systems?"

Dan was just staring down at his feet in silence.

DS Iqbal then gave Dan some more news, "Well, we have also obtained evidence that since you two joined the animal park, there has been a big spike in unaccounted for food and drink, which seems to have been disappearing from the kitchen. Hmm... neither of you are allowed in the kitchen, are you?"

"No, but we've done nothing wrong!" exclaimed Dan, who was now starting to feel a bit flustered.

"Interestingly, our colleagues have been watching the CCTV footage on every evening when Stan and you turned off and turned on the CCTV system. The enclosure keys that Stan and you always dropped on that table never moved during the period when the CCTV and alarm systems had been switched off except on the evening when the crocodile vanished. Do you have any explanation for that?"

Dan reverted to silence; this time half-closing his downward-looking eyes.

"The other difference we have found between the evening the crocodile disappeared and every other evening Stan and you worked was, of course, that on the evening of his leaving, in his usual resting in the pond, there was the log, which was a similar size to the crocodile. It had been cut from the enclosure's walnut tree whilst the CCTV system was turned off, that branch had crocodile skin on it, and the doors to his enclosure were found unlocked the following morning. Anything to say about all of that?" wondered DS Iqbal.

"No, nothing at all. We've done nothing wrong," grunted Dan.

"Well," chuckled DS Iqbal. He glanced at DC Kohli. The right time had been reached.

DS Iqbal put a hand to his mouth in an exaggerated manner as if he was trying to understand some confusing information.

After a few seconds, he sighed and said, "Only Stan and you were there. Only you two turned the CCTV system on and off. Only you two turned the alarm system on and off. Only you two had the keys at these times. Food and drink only started going missing from that kitchen after you two began working at the animal park. Only you two were there when the keys moved on the table. Only you two were there when the crocodile was last seen in his enclosure. Only you two were there during the time when a branch was cut off the tree, put in the pond and was found to have crocodile scales on it."

"So," continued DS Iqbal, "it would seem that you two are the only people who were there. The evidence points to Stan and you burgling the enclosure and the kitchen to steal the crocodile and all that food and drink. But you say it was not you?"

"Sarge," interjected DC Kohli in mock urgency. "I'm sorry to interrupt, but you have forgotten one other suspect?"

DS Iqbal stopped and pretended to look shocked. "Who?"

Dan momentarily looked up in hope. It didn't last long.

"The crocodile, Sarge!" exclaimed DC Kohli. "But I suppose Stan and Dan might have been in a conspiracy with the crocodile. Do Stan or you speak crocodile, perhaps?"

"Of course not," blustered Dan. "That's ridiculous. You can't conspire with a crocodile."

"Quite right," said DS Iqbal. "Everybody KNOWS that; whether they have a LONG, GREEN, SCALY NOSE or otherwise. Your case must be that the crocodile did it alone then! Let's consider the crocodile option. So he must have SCALED the tree."

"Everybody KNOWS. LONG, GREEN, SCALY NOSE. SCALED the tree, Sarge," enjoined DC Kohli, adding dreadfully bad comic repetition to the over-emphasised appalling puns of his sergeant – just in case the luckless suspect or his lawyer had missed them the first time. They hadn't!

Dan started to sink into his chair. Dan's lawyer started sinking into her chair too. Over the years, she had watched a number of her clients endure this comic duo routine when they tried to deny what seemed the undeniable. The officers really did enjoy their work.

Too much! thought the guilty.

Fantastic! thought the good citizens of East Cornwall.

DS Iqbal followed with, "Weren't crocodiles around during the time of the dinosaurs? Maybe he used his DINO SAW to chop down the branch?"

DC Kohli interjected, "DINO SAW. That's great, Sarge."

DS Iqbal then used his comic pause speciality. Raising his right forefinger into the air, as if he was checking the wind direction, he waited a few seconds. Dan stared at his finger wondering what was going on.

DS Iqbal then spoke, "Ah, I see now. The crocodile must have taken against Stan and you for some unknown reason and set you up! On every shift you two did for about a month, this crocodile must have SCALED that massive glass wall, he must have managed to get the kitchen's keys, open up the kitchen, go into it, SNAP up loads of food and drink, close it up, return the kitchen's keys and then SCALE back into his enclosure to lie down in his pond. He managed to do all of that in about a quarter of an hour, day after day. No wonder he needed to lie down for so long, he must have been tired out. And you two managed to miss it all!"

"SCALED! SNAP! Those glass walls are like slippery, see-through cliffs. Are you saying that the crocodile was a professional rock climber in his spare time? A ROCKODILE perhaps?" interjected DC Kohli.

"You may have a point there, DC Kohli. And no one, not even the CCTV, saw him move or do any of this, ever," reflected DS Iqbal.

The interview room fell into silence momentarily before DS Iqbal ended the quiet interlude with a snort.

"Oh, I get it now. You must be saying he was a MAGIC ROCKODILE!" exclaimed DS Iqbal.

Dan sunk even lower into his chair, as if he was trying to drill his way into the padding of his seat to hide.

His lawyer glanced at him and thought to herself, *You're lucky. Once the police have finished with you, you can go back to your cell and get away from it. I've got to suffer it all over again with Stan! I don't get paid enough for this. Maybe I should apply for one of the now vacant evening jobs at the animal park!*

"But," pontificated DS Iqbal, "last night, the MAGIC ROCKODILE took his show to a new level. Something more astounding to get his TEETH into. Not content with two SCALINGS of massive, perpendicular, slippery walls per night, not content with his trips into a locked kitchen where he SNAPPED up loads of food and drink, last night he must have upped his wall SCALINGS to FOUR! When he first SCALED the wall, he must have SNAPPED up the enclosure keys as well,

SCALED back over with them, unlocked both doors, SCALED the wall again, dropped off the keys back where he had found them (but not quite in the right place to really stitch you up), and SCALED the wall for a FOURTH time to get back into his enclosure before unlocking and walking out of both doors, politely closing them behind him and then disappearing into thin air! All of this and he was still able to get into the kitchen where he SNAPPED up loads off food and drink!"

"TEETH, SCALINGS, SNAPPED, SCALED, SNAPPING. Sarge, you're in form today. Given all of that, not to mention his skills with locked doors and his brilliant disappearing act at the end, would that now make the crocodile a MAGIC ROCKODILE-LOCKODILE, Sarge?" asked the smirking DC Kohli.

"It seems so, DC Kohli! Oh, and in between all of that, he also managed to SCALE about five to six feet up a tree, SNAP off a two-feet-long branch, SNAP off some of his SCALES, put them onto that piece of tree, and put that wood exactly where he would usually lie!" continued the jubilant sergeant.

"SCALE! SNAP! SCALES! Maybe with all those teeth, the crocodile was also a tree surgeon or possibly a branch CHOPPER in his spare time? A CHOPPERDILE, perhaps? He certainly got his TEETH into a lot of things in just fifteen minutes last night, Sarge. He must have been a MAGIC CROCODILE-ROCKODILE-LOCKODILE-CHOPPERDILE, perhaps?" added DC Kohli merrily.

Please make it stop! thought Dan.

His lawyer was by now staring at the far wall imploring something, anything, to happen to bring this interview to an end.

There was a loud knock on the interview room door.

DI MacEwan entered. She was introduced to Dan and his lawyer. She had some news.

"Sorry to pop in just like this, but I thought you'd like to know that we've found the last two places where Dan and Stan worked together – you know, West Tamar Valley Hospital and West Tamar Valley Council," said DI MacEwan.

Dan and his lawyer perked up. They both felt relieved that someone had turned up to end the onslaught of dreadful humour from the comedy duo. They hoped it was a sensible senior officer bringing new evidence to the interview that might help Dan and Stan, because things were not looking good for them at that moment.

"Yes, we did work in those two places before getting our jobs at the animal park. Very good references we got too," smirked Dan.

"That's good to hear," exclaimed DI MacEwan brightly with a big grin.

Dan's lawyer spotted the change in her tone of voice and

the big grin immediately. She buried her head in her notes waiting for the bad news. Dan continued to smile with undue confidence – that was a big mistake.

DI MacEwan looked at Dan's happiness and moved to deliver the detectives' pre-planned and new evidential blow. DI MacEwan changed her expression in an instant and delivered this knockout in a matter-of-fact, almost deadpan, manner. This was in stark contrast to the comic duo, but it was equally effective.

DI MacEwan stated, "I wouldn't count on the hospital and council giving you good references any more. We and they have both done checks. Coincidentally, or not, Stan and you also worked early evening shifts together in both the hospital and the council near to kitchens, which were locked, alarmed and into which you both weren't allowed to enter. What is interesting, though, is that both of those two workplaces have now discovered that during the times you two were working for them (and only during those times) they had loads of unaccounted for food and drink disappear from their kitchens. Sounds familiar, doesn't it? Just like you two at the animal park, eh? And even more strangely at both of those places, the CCTV and alarms were turned off each night by Stan and you whilst you were both on duty for about fifteen minutes! Luckily, they still had all of the relevant CCTV and alarm evidence. We're still going through it all but it looks strikingly similar to what you were doing at the animal park before you moved onto crocodile stealing and skinning, eh? I must dash, lots more work to do, but I thought you needed to know this. Just to be fair, of course. I wonder if you, Dan, could help my colleagues understand all about this during the rest of your interview? You know, stuff like how and why it all happened, etc.?"

DI MacEwan concluded this devastating news for Dan by moving from an expressionless face to a massive, toothy grin coupled with an extravagant shrug of her shoulders.

As she left the interview room, DI MacEwan said, "Carry on, Detective Sergeant Iqbal and Detective Constable Kohli. I hope I did not spoil your flow."

Dan looked devastated. His lawyer thought the game was up for him. DS Iqbal and DC Kohli could barely contain their glee. These three detectives' interval interview plan had worked like a dream.

"I expect Dan would like to speak with his lawyer after that before we continue," beamed DS Iqbal.

"Yes, please," gasped Dan.

Dan staggered out of the interview room. His lawyer trudged behind slowly.

DS Iqbal and DC Kohli left the room too afterwards and went into an empty office to carry on their planning. They were very happy.

Mary Mermicorn had been watching what was going on.

She was not as happy as the detectives. It was dawning on her that she might have accidentally helped to prove to the satisfaction of the police, and thereafter the human courts, that Dan and Stan had burgled the crocodile enclosure to steal Crocky as well as burgling kitchens to steal food and drink. However, her mermicorn rules of conduct meant that there was nothing she could do but hope that the humans would eventually reach the correct conclusions.

About half an hour later, Dan and his lawyer shuffled back into the interview room. DS Iqbal and DC Kohli had returned there some minutes beforehand. They were more than eager and ready.

DS Iqbal continued just where they had left off before DI MacEwan had joined in with the interviewing.

"So are you saying that the MAGIC CROCODILE-ROCKODILE-LOCKERDILE-CHOPPERDILE somehow knew that Dan and you were going to work in the animal park before even you two did? Does that mean his MAGIC extended to PREMONITION skills?" asked DS Iqbal.

He carried on, "Or are you now claiming that this crocodile was somehow able to know all about you two; he knew where you had worked before you started at the animal park; he was able to travel MILES to and from his animal park enclosure to two different venues in East Cornwall on MULTIPLE occasions; and when he reached them, he was able to get into those premises, burgled and steal from their kitchens, get out, and return to his enclosure at the animal park without ever being discovered or seen by anyone, or on any CCTV system, on those MULTIPLE occasions?"

DS Iqbal finished his questioning in a flourish of mock sarcastic incredulity.

This was DC Iqbal's cue.

"Are you SCALING the heights of truth or are your denials nonsense, Dan? Are you saying that this crocodile has been in, out and shaking it all about over a wide area of East Cornwall for months like some kind of reptilian hokey-cokey? I've heard of some snakes being called ADDERS, but if this crocodile has been leaving and returning to his enclosure on all of these MULTIPLE occasions, he must be a new species: a MULTIPLIER crocodile, perhaps? Maybe I should get on the phone to the local zoo about this new discovery!" laughed DC Kohli.

Dan had felt a tiny bit better after talking with his lawyer during the second interview break. That mood had now more than vanished. Colour drained from his face. First he went white. Very quickly, he started to feel sick. Then his face took a decidedly pale-green hue. His lawyer buried her face grimly into her notes.

"Now, your denials would appear to be a bit of a tall TALE – rather than a horizontal TAIL, perhaps. I don't think you'd even half-persuade the newest, most GREEN recruit from any police college. If the evidence against you was building into a storm, you would be into the TEETH of a hurricane by now. Come on, SNAP out of your lying. The SCALE of your untruths is obvious to anyone. Don't SWIM against the current of real facts," stated DS Iqbal, ramming home the police's advantage.

"TALE, TAIL, GREEN, TEETH, SNAP, SCALE, SWIM," chuckled DC Kohli.

Dan could not take it anymore. His lawyer wanted to be anywhere else. She was even wishing that she had made that dentist's appointment for root canal work that she had been putting off for months so that one of her colleagues would have been dealing with this job instead of her.

Dan put his head in his hands and burst into tears. He then started to babble really quickly through his sobs, confessing what Stan and he had actually done.

He wailed, "We didn't steal or skin that crocodile. Honest! I swear. We really did lock those doors. I haven't a clue how they came to be open. I haven't a clue how the crocodile came to be skinned or disappear. I don't know how the keys moved on that table. All we did was agree to burgle kitchens where we worked for a bit of free food and drink. We only turned off the alarms and CCTV while we nicked, scoffed and drank. Honest! You must believe me!"

DS Iqbal and DC Kohli did not believe him, but they had his admissions to a conspiracy to burgle. The only issue was whether this conspiracy also included stealing and skinning the crocodile. They thought that they had more than enough evidence against Dan to prove that. They were now even more confident that they would have more than enough evidence against Stan as well once they had interviewed him.

They wrapped up interviewing Dan quickly and took him back to his cell. Once again in their careers, DS Iqbal and DC Kohli thought it was great to have this much fun and get paid for it!

Dan's confession was not so well received by his lawyer. He had not given her any prior notice that he was going to admit anything. She reacted to his capitulation silently and staring at the interview room's table, as her heart sank into her boots. She stayed in that position until the police officers ended the interview. It may have been over for Dan, but she knew that this was only part one for her. She still had to get through Stan's interview. Things were not going to get any better for Stan or for her. At that moment, she decided she really needed a new job!

Chapter Fifteen

Justice Moves in Mysterious Ways

Stan and his lawyer spent a very uncomfortable couple of hours with DS Iqbal and DC Kohli culminating in the full comic duo treatment. Stan's interview ended with him breaking down and confessing just as Dan had done earlier. Like Dan before him, Stan was then taken back to his cell to await developments.

Their lawyer went outside to her vehicle in the police car park, put on her radio and gathered her thoughts. Her boss had asked her to stay at the police station until any charging decision had been made. She picked up her now cold coffee, which she had left in her car's central console's cup holder. She noticed its tepid feel, pulled a disapproving face and put it down again rapidly. She turned on her laptop and was met by an urgent message from her boss. She opened it with a sense of foreboding, which was not misplaced. A colleague had just gone down with a sickness big and so her quiet office day, which she had planned for tomorrow to try to catch up with her ever-burgeoning caseload, was no more. One of her colleagues had been tasked to look after all of their law firm's clients at Plymouth Magistrates' Court tomorrow. That was the day of the week which was always that major court's busiest day. To make matters more unpleasant, the whole firm knew that the strictest, most pedantic and most miserable district judge in the whole of South West England was presiding there for the day. Her boss had ordered her to take over her colleague's duties at that court.

She banged her head onto the steering wheel in despair. This set off her car's horn and scared a song thrush half to death as it was struggling to remove a large and juicy earthworm from a nearby flowerbed. The bird was livid. The worm was ecstatic, as it burrowed to safety.

"That was a most fortuitously timed sickness bug," mused the despondent lawyer. "I hope he feels better soon. I'm sure he will – possibly almost as soon as he's told I'm doing his court tomorrow!"

She sat up, sighed and started loading her personal details onto a recruitment website offering professional assistance for those seeking a change of career.

Back in the police station, the moods of DS Iqbal and DC Kohli could not have been more different to that of the defence lawyer. They almost skipped into DI MacEwan's office to chat with her about the state of the case. DI MacEwan was also in an exceptionally good frame of mind and they all enjoyed a nice, fresh cup of tea together. These three detectives completed all of their paperwork and worked out their pitch to the local prosecutor. They were doing such an efficient and thorough job that they were able to finish this quite quickly. After quenching their thirsts with tea, they walked out of their grand police headquarters to the much smaller and more aesthetically modest building next door. This was where the East Cornwall Prosecution Department was based.

The Chief Constable and the Chief Prosecutor of East Cornwall had already spoken together about the events at the animal park. The chief prosecutor had assigned his most experienced lawyer to the case. She was Morag O'Hara. She had been working in her small open-planned office for most of the day waiting for the police to be ready to chat with her.

Morag O'Hara was not the only person with a professional interest waiting for the police investigations to bear fruit. The day had started as a very quiet one for news in East Cornwall and the whole of the UK. In fact, there had been no big news stories around for a few days. Many journalists were itching for anything notable to happen. They had column inches and airtime to fill.

News of Crocky's disappearance broke on social media initially. Within minutes, it had gone viral. Social media was filled with outrage, indignation and myriad theories swirling around. The idea that gained the most traction claimed that a gang of professional, exotic animal skin thieves had targeted a family-friendly, significant Cornish tourist attraction. This view even extended to claims that this gang had infiltrated the animal park's workforce so they could target the star animal in the park.

Local and national media journalists noticed this social media explosion. Local journalists knew the animal park well. Many national journalists had spent holidays in Cornwall and so they also knew about the animal park. In fact, many people from all over the UK have taken holidays in beautiful Cornwall and so a large number of the UK's population had either visited the animal park or knew people who had.

Suddenly, the local and national media had a big, human-interest story about a small, well-loved and uniquely talented animal disappearing from a family-friendly animal park in a beautiful, well-known and well-visited part of the UK to break the slow news boredom. The media started to inundate the local police and the local prosecution department with requests for information. Their switchboards could not cope with all of this media interest and their systems crashed. It was well after lunchtime before they were able to deal with all of the calls about Crocky. Both the police and the prosecution department were only able to do that because they created new, temporary, stand-alone and distinct phone numbers and contact points for media queries.

The media also began contacting many local people, including speaking with worried children, parents, local councillors and the local MP. Before long, national figures were being contacted by the media, including the Chief Prosecutor for England and even government ministers.

By mid-afternoon, urgent questions were being asked in the House of Commons and the disappearance of Crocky had become the lead item on nearly all national and local television channels, radio stations and digital news outlets. As the media interest and exposure grew, public interest and concern expanded. This resulted in a large, growing crowd assembling outside the animal park's closed main entrance.

It was evening when the three detectives walked into Morag O'Hara's office to brief her about the case. After nearly an hour, and more cups of tea, the police presentation came to an end. The officers looked at Morag O'Hara, who had been typing lots of notes as the police spoke. Ms O'Hara's fingers stopped moving on the keyboard and she stared at her screen. The room fell silent. All that could be heard was the dull sound of vacuuming elsewhere in the building. Ms O'Hara's legal mind was analysing and considering all of the evidence and information. After what seemed a very long time, but was in reality only about three minutes, Ms O'Hara leaned back on her chair. She looked at the detectives and smiled a broad smile.

"Well," she began. "Thank you, Officers. You've done your usual very good and thorough job here. We all know this story is on national and local TV, radio and other news outlets. Questions are being asked in parliament. It's all over social media. So there's no pressure!"

Everyone in Ms O'Hara's office laughed.

Morag O'Hara continued, "All we need to remember is this. If we mess this up, the next time we meet we'll all be looking for new jobs!"

She gave the detectives an enormous and mischievous

grin from ear to ear. Everyone then burst out into even louder laughter.

After a little while, Morag O'Hara composed herself; well, just about.

Through chuckles, she advised, "Officers, please charge them both with conspiracy to burgle their employers to steal from them. They've both admitted that offence. All they dispute is whether or not their agreement included burgling the crocodile's enclosure to take the crocodile for his skin. They will have to plead guilty to the conspiracy offence sooner or later. If they insist on claiming that they had nothing to do with stealing and skinning the poor crocodile, using their unique MAGIC CROCODILE, ROCKODILE or WHATEVER defence, the judge will certainly want to try that allegation as it would make a massive difference to their eventual sentence. It would be the difference between something like a suspended prison sentence and doing time – probably measured in years rather than in months."

Morag O'Hara's limited composure then began to break down, "Because it would only be a trial about how guilty they are, not a trial about whether they are guilty or innocent, the judge alone would hear it without a jury. Do you know which judge would be almost certain to hear the trial?"

Her eyes twinkled through tears of mirth, which had started to form in her eyes.

"No, but please tell us?" asked DI MacEwan.

Morag O'Hara answered, "Well, this is so high profile it will definitely be heard by the new top judge in Truro. The new Recorder of the Duchy of Cornwall is His Honour Ponsonby Wellington-Smythe QC, MA (Oxon), LLM (Cantab). He started here only last week."

Ms O'Hara continued, "I would not like to be in the shoes of our two suspects facing trial and sentencing by this judge."

"Why not?" asked DI MacEwan, intrigued.

"You see, I am the Wildlife and Zoological Parks Lead Prosecutor for East Cornwall. I've come across our new judge a few times. He's very serious and he's quite an authority on exotic animal smuggling and mistreatment. I've heard it joked that he hates animal abuse more than most crimes against humans," Ms O'Hara started to explain.

Morag O'Hara paused for a couple of seconds for dramatic effect and everyone chuckled.

She then gave the officers a huge grin and continued, "In fact, his aunt, who brought him up as a child, is Lady Lavinia Wellington-Smythe, the President of the English Exotic Creatures Charity; or EECC as it is more commonly known!"

She shouted out "EECC" — or should that be "EEK" as it sounded exactly the same — and waved her hands in the air in mock fright as if she had seen a ghost.

"EEK!" the four professionals then sang out very loudly in unison, waving their hands in the air before they burst out laughing very loudly together.

Tears of amusement were rolling down their cheeks when DC Kohli managed to splutter, "Those two will certainly be saying 'EEK' when they find out!"

That caused more raucous singing of 'EEK', hand waving and then some added banging on Morag O'Hara's desk.

There was only one other person in the building at this time. She was Cal, who was the new cleaner for the East Cornwall Prosecution Department. Like the learned judge, she was also a serious person. She lived with her husband and five sons. Those six family members were always messing around and never treated life with the gravity she thought it deserved. She liked going out to work to get away from their incessant silliness and to have some proper sensible time to herself. Therefore, she was not amused when she heard all of this semi-tuneful merriment going on.

Cal muttered to herself quietly, as if she were talking secretly to the last bin she was emptying, "What's with all of this laughing and fooling around here? My mum told me this would be a very quiet office, full of research and studying. I can barely hear myself think with all this messing about!"

The detectives left Morag O'Hara's office with their charging authorisation. They walked next door back to their police headquarters. They spoke with the custody sergeant and Dan and Stan were both charged with conspiring together and with others unknown to burgle their employers and steal from them.

Dan and Stan went to East Cornwall Magistrates' Court the next day. Their case was sent to Truro Crown Court and they ended up getting remanded in custody awaiting their trial. They were sent to a very unpleasant prison in the middle of an extremely bleak part of West Country moorland. When Dan and Stan were told about the judge who would hear their case, they did indeed say 'EEK', and much more besides, on numerous occasions.

Morag O'Hara's tactically astute charging decision worked as she had planned. Dan and Stan had to plead guilty to the cunningly devised conspiracy charge, but they continued to deny having anything to do with the disappearance of Crocky, let alone the taking of his skin. The new Recorder of the Duchy of Cornwall was really, really, interested in the case. He made sure he was the trial judge.

Mary watched these criminal proceedings roll on quite astounded. She hoped the judge would make the right decision at the trial, but he did not. The trial lasted just a day. At the end of it, His Honour decided that Dan and Stan had conspired to steal Crocky, they had conspired to take Crocky for his skin, and they were part of a wider conspiracy involving exotic animal skin traffickers. The most learned judge took his findings and added to them what Dan and Stan had already admitted. This exotic animal-loving judge was extremely well aware that this case had huge local and national public, political and media interest. He knew that his verdict had cemented Dan and Stan as the most unpopular criminals in the whole of the UK at that time. The judge wanted to make sure he passed the most appropriate sentence so he adjourned their case for a week to consider what he should do.

When the day of sentencing arrived, Truro Crown Court's public gallery was packed, but it was far too small for the huge public and media interest. This resulted in a large crowd gathering outside the court building and an impromptu media city sprung up there.

Dan and Stan walked into the dock to learn their fate. Their lawyers had warned them to expect the worst but all of those years of getting away with appalling behaviour meant that they still did not believe anything that bad would happen to them. The learned Recorder of the Duchy of Cornwall listened to all of the lawyers and then retired for an hour to consider everything before passing sentence.

When the judge returned to court, the silence was deafening in and out of the building as they awaited his decision. He sentenced both Dan and Stan to four years' imprisonment each. Gasps went around the listening public and press. Dan and Stan looked stunned. They were still reeling with the knowledge that they were going to prison for a long time when the judge followed up with banning them both from owning, keeping, looking after and working with animals for the rest of their lives. With that, the judge asked the dock officers to take Dan and Stan away to prison and left the court.

Mary Mermicorn did not know whether to be happy or upset about the result of the case. What she had done had played a key role in protecting Crocky and all animals from Dan and Stan forever. Their terms of imprisonment did in a way punish them properly for everything bad that they had done throughout their lives; including the very many things the police and courts did not know about. However, the human judge had given those penalties and protections based upon an incorrect judgment about what Dan and Stan had done.

Mary knew, though, that had the human judge interpreted the evidence about the case in front of him correctly, Dan and Stan would almost certainly not have gone to prison and she was sure that they would not have been given the animal-related prohibitions. This left her feeling morally conflicted, but there was nothing she was allowed to do about it.

Dan and Stan were taken from the court room into the holding cells' area below it. As they arrived, they were moaning and shouting loudly to each other that they had nothing to do with Crocky's disappearance, and that four years' imprisonment and a lifetime ban from having anything to do with animals, for merely stealing a bit of food and drink, was just too harsh and unfair.

Listening to their sonorous complaining was Cal, the new court cleaner. She had left her job at the East Cornwall Prosecution Department because of what she regarded as the raucous joking around there.

As she began to scrub the cells' toilets, she thought to herself, *Ridiculous, rowdy merriment over there. Noisy misery and overwhelming self-pity here. My word, where has the old-fashioned British stiff upper lip gone! Even if those two crooks are right, they should've learnt long ago that if you follow a path of crime, and deny stuff you've actually done, you shouldn't be surprised when you get blamed for things you didn't do. And you certainly shouldn't be shocked when nobody believes you, even if you are actually innocent for once! What goes around, comes around, as they say!*

Chapter Sixteen

Dam Builders

The legal proceedings against Dan and Stan lasted a few months. But what had happened to Crocky in the meantime?

As the human investigations had gone down such a wrong track, Crocky was completely safe from human searching as long as he kept his head down and out of the sight of any of them. This was exactly what he was doing at the River Otter.

Whilst the first day of the police investigations was in full swing, Crocky was finishing his third slice of Black Forest gateau at the Beavers' dining table.

"*SNAP, nom, nom, nom*. Gerhard and Steffi, you make such wonderful cake. How can I thank you for your hospitality?" asked Crocky, munching away.

"Why thank you, Crocky," replied Steffi very proudly. "We don't want a penny, but we could do with some help with the dam."

Gerhard added, "Yes, all that rain has caused us big problems. The weather is all right now, but we haven't had all the stormwater through yet."

Crocky was already planning his next move and this request could be very useful.

"Of course, my dear Gerhard and Steffi. I hear Easter Bunny Meadow is near here. Is that right? If so, we can't have that flooding!" Crocky asked, trying to sound like this was a purely innocent question.

The Beavers fell for it.

"There's no need to worry about that," both Gerhard and Steffi said together.

Steffi continued, "Easter Bunny Meadow is only about four hundred yards downstream from us; but on the other side of the river. Although it's called a meadow, it's really a massive complex under a meadow. No humans will ever find it and it will never flood because it has such incredible systems to protect it. All of us animals around here know it is there. The creatures there, including the Easter Bunny herself, are all really lovely."

Gerhard interjected, "Yes, they are. You know, they supply all of the Easter eggs for the whole of England from over there."

Steffi added, "Yes, they do. The Easter Bunny has similar complexes all over the globe. What happens here, though, is that every Easter Monday, after a busy day of chocolate delivering, they hold a massive party across the river for all of us local animals and the workers at the complex. The food is amazing and seems never-ending – particularly the chocolate."

That last comment really interested Crocky. He licked his lips at the thought.

"How do you get a job there?" asked Crocky.

"Just ask. Some say that chickens tend to be the best at egg design, but that is not always the case. They have some very talented lambs, bunnies and ducks in that department too. They have huge numbers of other jobs there as well – particularly in March with Easter coming up!" laughed Steffi.

"Great! I want to do something useful and settle down here as it is so lovely. I'll go there tomorrow and ask for a job, but not before we have sorted out this dam!" exclaimed Crocky.

"That's a really good idea and thank you for your offer to help us. We really appreciate it. Please stay with us tonight. It's the least we can do. When you get a job at Easter Bunny Meadow tomorrow, they will sort out your accommodation – it's a big perk of working there," added Gerhard.

Crocky readily agreed. A night staying at the Beaver household would mean dinner and, he earnestly hoped, more slices of Black Forest gateau.

"Now where's that dam?" asked Crocky.

Crocky and the whole Beaver family started working on

repairing, strengthening and improving the dam. The Beavers were trying to create a feature which would trap the largest trout and make it easy for them to walk along the dam and catch them. However, the beauty of this design was that it would also let the smaller and younger trout escape so that their fishing was sustainable. Unfortunately, the storms had brought a particular problem to their project. The floodwaters had washed downstream a large and bright orange traffic cone. That cone raced down the river, gaining speed in the fast currents, until it was unceremoniously and instantly stopped in its tracks by the dam. It hit the Beavers' work with such force that it jammed fast and deeply into the structure. It was stuck fast in exactly the spot where the trout catching and filtering system was being built.

The six young Beaver children, Anton, Emma, Elke, Friedrich, Johann and Ursula, were all trying to remove it without much success. They were getting more and more upset and irritated by the second.

Child beaver bickering is much like human child bickering. It soon escalated with Emma and Johann storming off in a huff, and the other four refusing to talk to them or each other. Their mum and dad had been trying to ignore their arguments in the forlorn hope that they would resolve themselves quickly. In their hearts, they knew that this was highly unlikely, but they clung to that remote possibility more out of parental necessity rather than expectation. Their children had kicked off their disputes just at the most inopportune moment where Steffi, Bernhard and Crocky needed to be paying their greatest and totally undivided attention to their work, lest they were to risk a catastrophic dam collapse. Steffi and Bernhard felt that they had no option but to let their children sort it out themselves. Of course, this idea backfired spectacularly. Once Steffi and Gerhard were able to leave their work safely, they then had to deal with a much larger falling out between their children. They then had to spend a large amount of time trying to hear, understand, calm down and then reconcile six different, tearful and angry points of view.

Crocky watched as the Beaver parents went over to their squabbling brood. He saw their initial efforts being rebuffed. He watched as Gerhard and Steffi became more and more frustrated and exasperated at their increasingly forlorn and futile efforts. In what seemed like no time at all, Crocky saw things degenerate into a full-blown eight-way argument.

Eager to get the dam finished as quickly as possible, so he could concentrate on eating dinner, going to bed and getting to Easter Bunny Meadow, Crocky decided to carry on working alone. He thought that if he could remove the traffic come, that might remove one area of stress for the children and calm things down. He jumped into the River Otter to see what he could do.

The first thing he noticed was the freezing cold water. Luckily, he was still wearing his feather-packed crocodile skin jacket, which did help a bit. Still, he certainly wanted to get out of there and warm up as soon as possible.

Crocky swam to where the cone was buried into the dam. Crocky saw that the cone's top had hit and penetrated the structure. As that happened, he observed that the top eight inches of the cone had been bent slightly back on itself. This meant that the cone was trapped, almost as if it had become part of the dam. It also caused a pocket of water to become trapped in the bent back section.

Crocky moved back a couple of feet to consider what he should do. He looked around. Suddenly, he noticed a small, young trout darting around. She was constantly prodding towards the top of the cone. She looked very upset and extremely worried. She seemed so pre-occupied that she had not even acknowledged Crocky's presence.

Crocky floated slowly a bit closer to the little fish. As he did so, he could hear her shouting desperately, "Tiny, are you all right? Speak to me, please!"

Crocky could see that this small fish was getting more and more upset and panicky by the second. Even as he came closer to her, she did not seem to notice he was there. Crocky decided to find out what was wrong.

"*Ahem, SNAP*. Excuse me, but what's up? Can I help?" Crocky asked.

The little trout glanced over her shoulder at Crocky, looked at the cone again, and then looked back at Crocky in a double take. This fish was Tina Trout. She was four years old and she had never seen a real-life crocodile before. She had heard about them in story books and at pre-school. She thought that they were supposed to be scary and they ate lots of things including fish. She also knew that they did not live in Devon! She glanced at the cone once more before giving Crocky a third look. This time, she was hoping that he was not really there. He was. Tina felt a surge of terror.

"Don't eat me please!" squeaked out Tina.

Crocky was taken aback. He had not even thought of eating her for a second. So far as he was concerned, fish needed to be cooked. His favourite fish dish was traditional British fish and chips. Tina was about as far away from that as he could imagine.

"*SNAP*, do you have any chips with you?" asked Crocky.

" No?" spluttered Tina, very confused.

"Well, in that case, I have no intention of eating you. I only eat cooked fish and chips; not raw fish on their own. Yuck! Anyway, I'm only three years old and you look a lot older and stronger than me. I'd have to be really silly even to think about such naughtiness. For certain, I don't want to get bashed up by you!" Crocky then gave a mock shiver and put up his two front legs in a 'hands up' surrender pose.

"Please don't bash me?" asked Crocky.

Tina thought about what Crocky had said. She was indeed older than him. She was certainly not cooked. There were no chips to be seen anywhere. Her mummy and daddy were always telling her that she was a strong Big Girl. She also believed that she was a lot tougher and more grown up than her twin brother Tiny, who was stuck in the sealed-off tip of the cone. That was what was causing her such consternation. Tina decided that what Crocky was saying seemed to be the truth. Whilst she had never previously considered that she was so tough she could scare a small crocodile, it all made sense to her now she had thought about it.

"OK, I won't bash you as long as you are good!" stated Tina, boldly.

"Thank you," Crocky replied in pretend relief. "What's up then?"

Tina thought for a second, looked back at the cone and then babbled towards Crocky, fighting back her sobs, "Me and my twin brother, Tiny, were playing. Then a big wave came up with this big cone thing and scooped us up. Then the cone stopped with a big bang. I fell out. Tiny went into the top bit. He's stuck there. I can't get him out. He can't get out. I don't know where Mummy and Daddy are..."

Tina burst into floods of tears.

"Don't worry," soothed Crocky. "I need to get the cone out of this dam because I'm fixing it for the Beavers. When I do that, your brother will be able to get out, but I need your help, please? Can you help me?"

Tina looked at Crocky, surprised at his request. Her tears slowed down a little bit.

"But how can I help? I've tried everything!" Tina's bottom lip started to quiver again.

"Ah, *SNAP*, you won't have tried this. I'm part of Crocky's Sea and River Rescue Service. I'm trained to do this type of thing, but I can only do it with the right help," Crocky told Tina.

He was trying to make sure she calmed down and moved far enough away to let him detach the cone safely without hurting her.

He continued, "I need your strength to help me move this cone. I can't do it by myself, but I can do it with your help. You know, team work makes the dream work!"

Crocky looked at Tina hoping her family or nursery used that phrase. He saw the young fish smile weakly and nod her head slightly so he thought she understood what he was saying.

Crocky asked Tina, "Please swim past me and go to the end of my tail. Then please point your fins at my tail and send all of your power into me by shouting, '*ZAP*' as loudly as you can. Let's practice your shout first. Please shout '*ZAP*' on a count of three. One, two, there..."

Silence. Tiny had stopped crying but was staring at Crocky in bewilderment.

"What was that? Oh no, I'm going weaker," said Crocky as he pretended to go floppy. "Please shout 'ZAP' as loudly as you can to get my strength back up. One, two, three…" Crocky made himself super floppy. His plan worked.

"ZAP!" half-shouted the confused Tina. Crocky suddenly straightened up.

"Well done! You are so strong. Just your shout alone without you ZAPPING my tail has worked loads. I'm sure if you swim past me, shout 'ZAP' as loudly as you can, and point towards the end of my tail with all of your fins, your superstrength powers will fly into me and we will free your brother!" exclaimed Crocky.

Tina suddenly felt helpful and more determined than ever. She swam past Crocky, away from the cone and stopped behind his tail.

"OK. Here we go. On the count of three. One, two, THREE!" shouted Crocky as loudly as he could for the final bit of encouragement.

The brave Tina screamed out, "ZAP" and pointed her fins right at the end of Crocky's tail as he had asked.

Immediately, Crocky rammed his head as far and as hard as he could into the cone and started the fastest crocodile spin that he could do. Tina threw herself back in amazement as huge spiralling waves flew from his tail.

Up on the dam, Crocky's actions also had a very useful effect. None of the arguing Beaver family members had noticed Crocky jumping into the river. Their arguments came to an abrupt halt because Crocky's spinning made the dam shake and waves crash around them like a mixture of an earthquake and mini tsunami. Gerhard and Steffi grabbed three children each and threw themselves off the dam onto the river bank as far away from the structure as possible. They cowered, fearing the worst.

Crocky's spinning worked. The cone broke free from the dam, leaving a small hole. Miraculously, this created the perfectly sized aperture for the Beaver family's fish trap system. The end of the cone flipped over, freeing a startled and very dizzy Tiny Trout. This young fish landed on Crocky's nose. The river's current caused the water to flow back towards Crocky and it stuck on the top of his head. Crocky saw Tiny starting to struggle against the water flow. As soon as Tiny was swept off Crocky's nose, he responded immediately, like Crocky's mother had done many years ago, by gently rescuing the little fish within his mouth. Crocky swam away from the dam into a slower flowing part of the river. As the waters calmed a bit, he felt a small fin touch his back.

Tina asked, "Is anyone underneath that big orange beak?"

That gave Crocky an idea – a most mischievous idea – but that would have to wait. He shook off the cone, opened his mouth and out swam a still dizzy and completely shocked Tiny.

"Tiny, you're safe!" shouted his overjoyed twin sister, throwing her fins around him.

Then they heard further shouting as their mummy and daddy came within three feet of Crocky. They had just witnessed within a short space of time their daughter talking to and ZAPPING a crocodile, that crocodile doing a really fast roll, and their son coming out of the crocodile's mouth. They were beside themselves in fear, worry and a thousand other emotions. Crocky quickly spotted their angst and realised immediately whom they were.

"My dear Mr and Mrs Trout. You have done a wonderful job in bringing up such brave, sensible, strong and caring children. They are a credit to you and themselves. They stayed strong for each other. If it wasn't for your daughter's calmness and 'ZAP', I would not have been able save her brother. If it wasn't for your son's calmness and strength in jumping into my mouth to escape his imprisonment, I would not have been able to save him either. They both acted better than any other superhero could have done. Please take your children back home and I hope you can find it within yourselves to find a little treat for such wonderful children," finished Crocky with a big grin.

Crocky then whispered to the Trout family, "Please don't come back down here by the dam. I am helping the Beaver family repair it, but they are putting in a trap for larger fish. Smaller fish will not get trapped here but these two fine children need their loving parents!"

Crocky then gave Mr and Mrs Trout a friendly wink.

Mr and Mrs Trout were flabbergasted. Not only had they never seen or met a crocodile in the River Otter, or anywhere else for that matter, but they had never expected to discover that any crocodiles could be so kind and considerate. They both shouted their thanks to Crocky and hugged him. Tiny gave him a shy small wave of a fin, when prompted by Mrs Trout. Tina saw what her brother had done and decided to outdo him in how she would show her thanks to Crocky.

Tina swam up to the crocodile and gave him a big kiss on his left cheek. Crocky fainted!

Crocky had never been kissed by anyone since his mummy last kissed him many years ago. That kiss happened on that fateful morning just after some humans had taken his daddy and shortly before they took his mummy. It was the last, loving, farewell kiss of a parent to their child. It was the day before his fourth birthday. It was the day he became an orphan. That was why, when asked his age, he always said he was three: to try to keep him closer to his parents and protect his few most precious memories of them. Being lovingly kissed by Tina reminded him of that final motherly kiss. It was far too much for his emotions.

The Trout family was very surprised and worried by this unexpected turn of events. They all fussed around Crocky and were most relieved when he came round. After a good few minutes of caring, checking and Crocky continually trying to reassure them that he was all right, the Trouts were finally happy that they could leave him and he would be safe. Crocky watched them swim home, which was only a couple of hundred yards away upstream. Their home was in an idyllic spot beneath an overhanging, ancient willow tree, whose spring green branches were brushing the water surface below.

Crocky turned away and saw that the traffic cone had floated to the bank on the Easter Bunny Meadow side of the river. He went over to the cone, dragged it onto dry land and broke off its tip with his teeth. Crocky opened his crocodile skin jacket and placed the tip within it. He then went over to the dam to meet the Beaver family, who had ended their arguing and decided that they were now safe. As he approached them and were now standing on top of the structure, the Beaver family were marvelling at how Crocky had managed to create the perfect-sized hole for their larger fish trap when he removed the cone.

All nine animals quickly settled back to work and managed to complete the dam's repairs and improvements by the late afternoon, as daylight was starting to fade.

"Would you like to try some Steckelfisch?" asked Gerhard

as they were tidying up.

Crocky looked at him quizzically. He did not want to say he had no idea what Gerhard was talking about because he did not want to appear rude or ignorant.

Steffi intuitively noticed that Crocky was unsure about her husband's request so she interjected, "Bavarian fish on a stick. We put a fish on a stick, a bit like a barbecue stick, and grill it. It could be any type of fish but around here, like it was in our old home in Bavaria, it is trout. Before we grill the fish we flavour it with a marinade. We have a large variety of scrummy marinades. Once we've eaten enough fish, we move on to the gateau. Does that sound all right for you, Crocky?"

"Steckelfisch and gateau, yes please!" chorused their six children.

"*Yum, yum, yum, SNAP!*" exclaimed Crocky. "You and your children have sold it to me!"

Everyone laughed.

The nine friends then spent a lovely evening eating, chatting, laughing and celebrating the completion of the dam, before they all settled into a happy and contented sleep.

Chapter Seventeen

Crocky Reaches Easter Bunny Meadow

Early next morning, Crocky awoke. After a hearty breakfast of six large Danish pastries, he said his goodbyes to the Beaver household and set off for Easter Bunny Meadow to find work. It was another fine morning but still quite chilly. In a few patches, Jack Frost had left a little sprinkling of his special icing sugar. Crocky noticed it was crunchy underfoot, so he took extra care. He did not want to stumble or slip, particularly as he crossed the newly repaired and upgraded dam.

As he passed over that structure, he glanced down at his handiwork and smiled to himself in self-congratulation. He made his way onto the opposite riverbank, before walking slowly out of the view of the Beaver household. Crocky saw a small copse of trees and bushes ahead of him and walked into it. As the frost had not permeated beneath the branches and foliage, Crocky was able to walk with a great deal more speed and ease in there. When he was certain that he was hidden so well that he could not possibly be seen, he stopped. He took off his crocodile skin jacket and sat down upon a fallen tree trunk.

Crocky spent the next few hours diligently and meticulously weaving most of the feathers that he had kept inside his jacket onto the outside of it. Then he removed the jacket's sleeves, which had covered his front legs. This left two holes at the top of the jacket, which he concealed with larger feathers. Those two detached jacket sleeves were not wasted. Crocky stitched them to the bottom of the sleeves that had covered his hind legs to lengthen them. He stitched feathers into these extended sleeves too.

Crocky stretched and altered the collar of his jacket to make a large hood, which covered the whole of his head apart from his nose and mouth. He put feathers into this head covering as well. He ensured that he had stretched the bottom of his jacket so that he could conceal his whole tail within it.

Crocky knew that for his chicken disguise to have any chance of working, he would have to use his meerkat trick and walk on his hind legs only. This left him with the huge problem of what to do with his front legs. He could not make them look like wings in any realistic way. He decided to hide his front legs inside his jacket and have no wings. He hoped that anyone who saw him would either not notice or they would be too polite to make any comment about it.

Once Crocky had completed the transformation of his jacket, he took hold of the tip of the traffic cone, which he had kept. Crocky used his teeth to mould it so that it hid all of his teeth and it also fit perfectly around his nose and mouth. This gave Crocky the appearance of having a long, but well-used, beak.

"Thank you, Tina, for the beak idea," muttered Crocky to himself as he came out of the copse.

He went in a crocodile and came out a rather peculiar and scruffy-looking chicken. He looked at his reflection in a slower part of the river and smiled to himself.

"*CLUCK, CLUCK, CLUCK,*" he practised. Occasionally, he said, "*SNAP*", but he quickly taught himself to turn that into a cough-type sound. Now his disguise was complete, it was time to get a job with the Easter Bunny. He walked along the riverbank towards his goal.

Chocolate; mountains of chocolate, thought Crocky to himself. *Now to make up for missing all of that Christmas confectionary with Easter choccy.*

As Crocky entered the field under which Easter Bunny Meadow was situated, he met Chomper. He was very surprised to see a chicken with teeth. For a split second, he wondered if it would be all right if he showed her his teeth because the cone disguise was a bit uncomfortable, but very quickly he thought better of that idea.

"Err, *sna—cough.* Excuse me. I'm quite new around this area. I've just arrived from Cornwall and need some work. Are there any jobs here please?" asked Crocky.

Mary Mermicorn had been keeping herself well aware of what Crocky was doing. She thought that if he was able to get a permanent job at Easter Bunny Meadow, then in spite of his current ideas he would have no need to steal anything because of the abundant food there. Further, she knew that as long as he lived and worked for the Easter Bunny, he would never be found by any humans. Therefore, he would never be at any risk of harm by them. As a result, she decided to use her magic to help him make his disguise and, in spite of his strange appearance, she ensured that no one at Easter Bunny Meadow would believe that Crocky was anything other than a real chicken.

Chomper looked at him. She had never seen such a peculiar-looking chicken before. Then she noticed that Crocky did not appear to have any wings.

"Good morning," Chomper said. "Please come with me to see if there are any jobs for you here at Easter Bunny Meadow. There are usually a number of jobs at this time of year. I hope you don't mind me asking, but what happened to your wings?"

Crocky's wings plan has failed at the first obstacle. He paused before replying, desperately trying to think of something plausible to say. Then he had a brainwave.

"Oh, *sniff, sniff,*" began Crocky pretending to be fighting back tears. "I'm sorry but that question has brought back such terrible memories. You see, I lost my wings to a fox."

Chomper fell for Crocky's acting. She knew all about how horrible foxes could be to chickens. She felt really dreadful for asking Crocky such a painful and insensitive question.

"I'm so sorry to hear that and I'm really sorry to have

upset you. It was never my intention. I know all about naughty foxes. I did not mean to make you cry. I just want to help you get the most suitable job. What's your name?" babbled Chomper, trying to recover from her feelings of discomfort.

"You're too kind," said Crocky magnanimously through a few more sniffs. "My name is, SN.–cough, Clucky. Clucky Diall."

He then spelt out his new name trying hard to keep a straight face. As soon as Chomper asked him for his name, he realised he had forgotten that simple but important detail. You could not really have a chicken called 'Crocky'!

Clucky Diall was the best name, and the only name, that Crocky was able to come up with when he was put on the spot like that. He just hoped he would be able to remember it.

"That's a nice name," said Chomper politely. "Please follow me."

At being told this name was nice, Crocky was really glad his face was covered with feathers and part of a traffic cone to help him hide and stifle the giggles.

Chomper led the way up to a tree stump, which was situated a few hundred yards away from where they had met. She tapped it with her beak. Crocky noticed that a large section of grass, which was a further ten yards beyond the tree stump, started to shake. He saw the ground part. This revealed a large and brightly lit hole. Within that hole, Crocky could see a wide pathway descending and disappearing deep into the ground.

"Follow me to the reception, please," said Chomper.

Chomper skipped off ahead into the hole. Crocky followed immediately behind her. As soon as they were both inside, Crocky noticed the entrance closing silently behind them.

Chapter Eighteen

The Easter Bunny's Global Enterprise

Just as Steffi Beaver had told Crocky, Easter Bunny Meadow was a huge underground complex, but it was only one part of a worldwide system.

How these complexes came about arose from an unlikely beginning. The Easter Bunny had an extremely close friendship with the Tooth Fairy. Many years ago, a few weeks after Easter, they were both at a party when the Tooth Fairy asked the Easter Bunny about how Easter had gone for her.

The Easter Bunny said it had gone well, but she was becoming concerned about the Earth's increasing human population. She told her friend that she was trying to work out a way to make it easier for her to deliver Easter eggs to more and more people.

At that time, the Easter Bunny worked from a single secret location. This was great for delivering to places near it, but it was very inefficient for getting to locations on the opposite side of the world. The Easter Bunny had some inherent magical powers that helped her but they were limited to things like speed, strength, invisibility and memory.

However, the Easter Bunny could also see that whilst it was not ideal to have to serve the growing number of people on Earth from a single place, it was still really useful to have one centre of expertise to make and develop her chocolate creations. This was a conundrum that she was having great problems solving. She opened up her feelings and concerns to the Tooth Fairy. The Tooth Fairy listened carefully and kindly. After a short pause, the Tooth Fairy suggested that they find a quiet corner and stay there until they had worked out what had to be done.

That is what they did. For the rest of the party, and for a few hours beyond, they sat in that corner discussing, laughing, thinking and finally agreeing what should happen. Their answer was incredible in its scale and complexity, but it worked.

Their idea was a truly global Easter Egg Enterprise, which kept the benefits of a single centre of expertise, but which also had an equitable and efficient worldwide reach. It was something that would be environmentally friendly and, most importantly, the humans would never discover it. They decided to move the Easter Bunny's secret centre into the Earth's core. That location was perfect. It was roughly equidistant from everywhere on the Earth's surface. The Tooth Fairy's magic was much more extensive than that of the Easter Bunny and so she turned the fire and incredible heat of the core from a massive problem into a huge benefit.

Firstly, the Earth's core is so inhospitable that it is impossible for any humans or any of their technology to go or function there. That meant that regardless of the Easter Bunny's powers of making things invisible, no human would ever find or even think of looking for the Easter Bunny's central workplace at that location.

Secondly, the core's never-ending heat and fire would provide all of the energy that the Easter Bunny's operations centre would ever need with no harmful emissions.

The Tooth Fairy used her magic to create an enormous, indestructible, hollow Easter-Egg-shaped building right in the middle of this supercharged furnace. She transported the whole of the Easter Bunny's secret centre into it. The Tooth Fairy created unbreakable power systems that used and re-used the Earth's core's energy to power all of the Easter Bunny's works all over the world.

Once the chocolate was being made at the core, the Easter Bunny and the Tooth Fairy had to get it to the surface as quickly and efficiently as possible for the most effective global distribution service. They did this by using the Tooth Fairy's magic to create a worldwide network of huge distribution and supply hubs – just like the one by the River Otter in Devon. The centre of operations and all of these hubs were linked by the Bunny Burrow Railway – or BB as it was known affectionately by her English-speaking staff. The BB was a mixture of an underground train network and a teleportation system. It allowed for light-speed travel between all of the Easter Bunny's premises wherever they were. It could carry passengers or goods. It was the key component that allowed huge quantities of chocolate to be made in the Earth's core and shipped to all four corners of the globe almost instantaneously. It also enabled the Easter Bunny and her staff to move all over the world at incredible speeds whenever that was needed. This was particularly invaluable in the early hours of Easter Sunday.

The Easter Bunny's magical powers of invisibility ensured that all of these new hubs were never discovered by any humans.

The Easter Bunny needed a very large global workforce, who could do their jobs happily and safely, without any humans finding them or where they were employed. The obvious answer was to make all of the hubs and the centre big enough for the whole workforce to live and work within them. However, the Tooth Fairy and the Easter Bunny knew that it would be most unhealthy for the vast majority of the workforce to spend nearly all of their time underground, missing out on sunlight and all of nature's overground necessities of life.

The Tooth Fairy resolved this by bringing the surface conditions underground. The details she put into this were incredible. She made all of the hubs and the centre, whether they were work or non-work areas, the most beautiful and practical places possible. They reflected the finest countryside and architecture of the countries or regions under which they were built. In all of these underground spaces, the Tooth Fairy used her magic to make real sunlight shine, real weather conditions occur, the seasons change and real sky scenes – including sunrises, sunsets, night skies and the phases of the moon. She did all of this to mirror the conditions occurring immediately above them in the open air.

The Easter Bunny thought all of these plans were wonderful, but she had concerns about exactly matching the weather conditions that were happening above ground within her underground complexes. The Easter Bunny spoke about her worries with the Tooth Fairy.

She said, "It's great to match conditions above and below, but I don't think we should have an underground hurricane just because there was one on the surface."

The Tooth Fairy agreed. They could not do anything to harm the health, safety and comfort of the Easter Bunny's colleagues. So they agreed to temper all weather extremes. So, if there was a hurricane above one of the Easter Bunny's complexes, it would only be moderately breezy and rainy underground.

As the core was directly below everywhere on Earth, it could have had the climate and conditions of anywhere. After much thought, the Easter Bunny decided to give it a similar climate and setting to the Devon hub.

The Easter Bunny explained her reasoning to the Tooth Fairy, "Devon is beautiful. Its climate is wonderful because of its variety. Nature has decided that Devon gets most of the weather types that we see all around the world; but it does not often get them in the most extreme ways. After all, we seldom get Saharan heat waves, Artic winter storms, Caribbean hurricanes, Asian monsoons or Australian hailstorms in

Devon."

She continued whilst starting to chuckle, "Also, it will remind me of my favourite food treat. I love West Country Cream Teas; particularly with carrot cake!"

When all of this work was completed, the Tooth Fairy told the Easter Bunny that she did not have the time to help her run her chocolate empire permanently as she had so many teeth to collect and pennies to leave each night. The Tooth Fairy knew that running such a major organisation with limited magical abilities would be nearly impossible for the Easter Bunny, so for the first and only time she cast a spell giving to the Easter Bunny all of the Tooth Fairy's magical abilities.

The only caveats were that the Easter Bunny could not change or scrap any spells cast by the Tooth Fairy without her express permission and the Easter Bunny would lose all of these new powers if she ever abused them. But this was the Easter Bunny, so that was never going to happen!

Chapter Nineteen

Clucky Diall Starts Work

Crocky followed Chomper to the Devon hub's reception. On the way there, he saw a number of animals moving around. They were working hard but happily. In the background, he could smell a slight aroma of chocolate.

He just managed to stop himself saying out loud, "*Yum, yum, yum, SNAP!*"

Gordon Gannet was the receptionist and a recruiter. After Crocky was introduced by Chomper, Gordon asked him what experience he had and what job he wanted to do.

"Due to the attack with the fox – he ate my wings, which you can probably see – I have found it impossible to get any jobs. That's why I came here because I heard of the Easter Bunny's reputation for equality, and treating all on the basis of their abilities, not focussing on their disabilities," stated Crocky staccato style through a few sniffs. He hoped he had remembered enough of the various Human Resources chats he had heard people having over cups of tea near to his enclosure at the animal park.

The reaction of Gordon made him confident that he had managed to strike the right note.

"Definitely. Only Santa's North Pole centre has a similar

level of genuine equality of opportunities as here," smiled Gordon. "We are currently really short of workers in the warehouse. We have machinery that I am confident you will be able to operate and be a real asset to us. You will be helping to move huge quantities of chocolate into and out of here for the whole of England. You'll get free board and lodgings, regular breaks, and the usual fair wage. You will also be enrolled into the Warehouse Union unless you wish to opt out – but no one here does because the Easter Bunny and the unions work so well together – and the free union parties are legendary!"

"Brilliant! Sign me up for everything please. When do I start?" rattled off Crocky in joyous excitement.

Gordon Gannet grinned at Crocky, opened a desk drawer and took out a draft contract of work for Crocky to sign.

Gordon said, "That's great. Let's sort out the paperwork and then you can start immediately."

Gordon and Crocky spent the next hour making sure everything was signed and agreed. As they were doing this, Mary Mermicorn was watching. She was very pleased.

Mary thought to herself, *Why would Crocky want to throw away all of this permanent free board and lodgings, which would allow him to eat large amounts of human food, including chocolate, for short-term stealing?*

After all of the administrative paper filling, signing and

copying had been completed, Crocky was a full-time worker for the Easter Bunny. As he was smiling about his successful enrolment, Crocky heard the sound of pawsteps approaching him from behind. Crocky turned around and saw a jolly-looking grey and white furred rabbit approaching. For a moment, Crocky wondered if this was the Easter Bunny, but he concluded that it probably wasn't.

The rabbit spoke in a loud and friendly way, "Welcome, welcome to Easter Bunny Meadow's Warehouse Department. I'm Con Veenor. You must be Clucky Diall?"

"Yes, that's right. But please call me Clucky," replied Crocky.

"Clucky, it's a pleasure to meet you. I love seeing new people join our happy band. I've been working in these warehouses for over twenty-five years. I've loved every minute of it! I've been head of the Warehouse Union for twenty of those years. The warehouses are a great place to be. We have wonderful colleagues. You'll have a great time here!" said Con with seemingly boundless energy.

Con then changed his tone and spoke a little more softly and slowly, "I'm sorry to hear about your wings. Foxes, eh? I must let you know straight away that we do have foxes working all over Easter Bunny Meadow and elsewhere in the Easter Bunny's business centres so you will see some of them. They are all very nice and would not dream of doing anything unpleasant to anyone; but if you have any issues, please let me know and I will try to sort something out for you."

"Thank you for the warning and your kind words, *SN–cough*. I don't think I'll have any problems with colleagues here. It's wild foxes I have issues with!" replied Crocky.

Con pointed to a mark on the left-hand side of his nose and said, "See that scar there? Caused by a fox when I was a young bunny. He tried to get my tail next, but my strong back legs gave him a nose bleed to remember. I escaped down a nearby rabbit hole!"

The mention of a tail made Crocky realise that he had forgotten to give himself any tail feathers. This fox conversation gave him a splendid idea to deal with that before anyone noticed.

Crocky replied very quickly, "That was a good thumping you gave that fox and a lucky escape. In spite of losing my wings and my tail feathers, which were so damaged they never grew back..."

At that, he spun around and gave Con a flamboyant wiggle of his bottom to highlight the point.

"... in many ways I was the lucky one," continued Crocky. He was enjoying embellishing his invented backstory. "If you'll pardon this pun, at least I survived to tell the tale, *SN–cough*... ho, ho!"

"Yes, I've lost a few bunny friends over the years to foxes. I know exactly what you mean. You're quite right; often it's better to focus on what you have rather than what you've lost," pondered Con philosophically.

Con looked briefly towards Gordon and thanked him for enrolling Crocky before turning his attention back to the new employer.

"Follow me, Clucky. Let's get started!" stated Con with more than a hint of urgency.

With that, Con marched out of the reception at speed. Crocky followed as fast as he could in his disguise. He was feeling very pleased with himself.

They soon reached a large open space and stopped. Con took out a small device that looked a bit like a mobile phone and said into it, "Train for two, please."

There was a small flash and a slight pop sound. At once, right in front of them, there appeared a small, single carriage train containing two large seats only. It had no driver. On its side nearest the two animals there was a large door, which was already open.

Crocky was shocked. He looked around blinking, trying to make sense of this train's sudden appearance. There were no tracks. There was no station announcer. In fact, there was no station. Crocky was really confused.

"This is the Bunny Burrow Railway," explained Con. "Everybody calls it the BB. It's how all of us and all of our freight move around and between all of the Easter Bunny's complexes throughout the world. When we get to the warehouses, I'll give you a phone. You can use that to call up BBs, I mean trains, of any size or type (passenger or goods), whenever you want. You must be polite. The BB is a stickler for politeness and will not work for anyone who is disrespectful, impolite or downright rude. All you have to do is ask the BB for the train you want on your allocated phone. When it arrives, you just have to tell it where you want to go. As long as your request is fair, reasonable, justified and, I must re-emphasise, POLITE, the BB will get you the train you need, and it will take you exactly where you want to go instantaneously. Come along, let's jump aboard."

Con and Crocky hopped onto the train and sat down. The seats were really comfortable. Crocky settled down contemplating if he might have time for a snooze. He didn't.

Con spoke into his phone, "Warehouse Zone C, please."

The large door closed and at once there was a slight pop sound, another small flash and the view outside changed completely. The train had stopped outside an immense warehouse, which was designed to resemble an inspiring ecclesiastical building. Next to that building were many other similarly sized warehouses each with designs ranging from country houses to grand railway stations, from town halls to historic waterfront buildings, and many more quintessentially English architectural styles. They were set in an attractive, undulating landscape of trees, streams, small lakes, fields and the appearance of moorland-topped hills in the distance.

The train's door opened and Con jumped out.

"Come on, Clucky. We are here now. Let's show you what you are going to do."

Crocky alighted from the train and looked up. Now he was outside the carriage he was able to get a better perspective of the scale of everything. He gasped in awe. The warehouses seemed to stretch into the upper limits of the sky and as far as the eye could see into the distance.

They walked towards the nearest warehouse.

"It looks just like a church; maybe even a cathedral from the outside," said Crocky.

"Yes, it does. It's actually based upon beautiful Exeter Cathedral. It's not just the outside either. When we go inside, you will see stained glass windows and a stone ceiling. Exeter Cathedral has the longest uninterrupted medieval stone vaulted ceiling in the world. There are lots of clocks – taking their colours and themes from Exeter's lovely astronomical clock. You will also see loads of the most beautiful, fine, ornate woodwork made from finest Devonian oak," enthused Con.

Crocky and Con entered the warehouse through wonderfully carved huge oak doors showing numerous spring flowers and baby creatures. Crocky immediately saw that Con was not overstating the magnificence of the interior. Whilst it was a huge and completely practical working warehouse, the inside was just as ornate and aesthetically attractive as the outside. There seemed to be endless rows and shelving, many wide aisles and countless pieces of machinery and animals everywhere. Deliveries were being made to the sides of the warehouse by multiple goods trains through enormous openings.

"Wow," muttered Crocky to himself at this wondrous hive of activity.

Con shouted across to a small figure, who was standing a couple of aisles away from where they were. He looked up, flashed a huge, dazzlingly white-toothy smile and waddled over to greet them.

This was Mylo Jystics. He was a small, studious-looking mole. He had delicate round glasses perched towards the bottom of his pointed nose. He wore an extremely dapper, black and velvety three-piece suit. In the left pocket of Mylo's waistcoat, Crocky could see that he had a glinting, silver pocket watch just peeking out. An equally sparkling fob ran from the top of that watch like a gentle wave with sparkling links rising to crest at the waistcoat's middle button hole before descending seamlessly into his pocket on his right.

Beneath his waistcoat, Mylo wore a startlingly white, double-cuffed, stiffly starched, wing-collared shirt. His cuffs were kept together with handcrafted cufflinks made from finest Welsh gold. Upon each of those cufflinks was a small shield. One of those shields bore the picture of a mole dressed as a medieval knight. The other shield had within it the image of a mole attired like a court jester.

Around his neck, Mylo wore an oversized and extravagant bow tie. Its main colour was a vivid and sharp yellow. Just in case that was not garish enough, upon that yellow were scattered numerous, large, fluorescent and bright polka dots; half of those dots were lime green and the other half were carnation pink.

Upon Mylo's feet were the most highly polished, finest, black, faux leather shoes. Crocky thought you could have used his shoes as mirrors.

"Hello, Mylo. Meet Clucky, our new recruit. Could you fix him up with a phone, a computer pad, show him what to do and point him in the right direction, please?" asked Con.

Mylo flicked back his head and glanced at Crocky. He then flashed Crocky a cheeky smile and winked at him.

Mylo looked back at Con and replied, "My dearest Con. It's so nice to see you. And you've come along with another newbie for me. How kind. Of course I'd LOVE to FIX him up. I'd LOVE to SHOW him what to do. I just hope that after all of that

I will still have the energy to POINT him in the right direction!"

Mylo finished speaking by pulling a silly face. Crocky could see that Mylo was not the most staid or serious of creatures, but he liked his humour. He started to laugh.

Con, though, pretended not to be amused. He gave a large sigh and rolled his eyes.

Con said to Crocky, "As you can probably tell by his level of so-called humour, Mylo loves the stage, particularly Christmas pantos. Last Christmas, he was one of Cinderella's ugly sisters in the Easter Bunny Meadow's show. He's already practising for Widow Twankey in Aladdin for next Christmas!"

"Oh no, I'm not!" called Mylo.

"Oh yes you are!" chorused Con and numerous other workers around the warehouse.

Laughter started to echo and grow throughout the building.

Whilst the chuckling continued, Crocky's induction into his job started in earnest. He was going to be a driver of a Hare Hopper – known as an HH.

An HH was very similar to a huge forklift truck. His job was to drive it to the side of the warehouse to meet BB goods trains as they arrived loaded with Easter eggs and other Easter chocolate. Those items of chocolate were called EEs, which stood for Easter eggs, which was the main chocolatey design in England.

The EEs were transported by the trains in huge pallets. His HH would drive to the BB, remove a pallet of EEs and 'hop' them across into the appropriate and extremely large containers within the warehouse. These enormous containers were stacked on what looked like huge shelving units, which seemed to fill the warehouse to the roof and from side to side as far as Crocky's eyes could see. These containers were officially called Coney Containers, but the workers, of course, called them CCs. They were organised simply on the basis of where in England the EEs were going to be delivered. For example, one CC could contain all of the Easter eggs for Peterborough, whilst another could contain all of the Easter eggs for Runcorn and so on. In some ways, it was just like an enormous mail sorting office, but dealing with chocolate instead of letters and parcels.

Crocky was handed a laptop and a mobile phone. He was told that all he had to do was go to the nearest HH at the start of his shift. As soon as he sat on the driver's seat and placed his laptop on a small shelf to the left of him, that device would automatically link up with the HH and start the work programmed for Crocky to do that day. The HH would then do all of the day's work without Crocky having to do anything at all but keep a look-out.

Well, that was the theory. However, the Easter Bunny

knew that even the best automated systems could sometimes go wrong. So the Easter Bunny made sure that all HHs had drivers. Their roles were actually more health and safety, or troubleshooting, because they did not drive the HHs at all. In the unlikely event that something went wrong, they would try to stop it or fix it.

The HH had a stop peddle and a stop button. Either one would make the device stop immediately. Crocky's mobile phone was another safety device to deal with any issues. If the laptop failed, or if something unexpected happened that needed Crocky's intervention away from the programmed routine, all Crocky needed to do was give a command starting with the word "phone" and his mobile phone would override his laptop's instructions. That was why it did not matter that Clucky did not have any wings for this job.

Mylo explained to Crocky that on the night before Easter, the EEs would be teleported to the Racing Rabbit – or RR – for delivery. Racing Rabbit or RR was what the Easter Bunny was affectionately, and very aptly, called on that ever-so-busy night only.

Mylo finished his induction; or that was what Crocky thought.

As Con had said, Mylo loved pantomimes. For one so small in stature, he had a larger-than-life theatrical personality. He loved playing the villain or a pantomime dame. He also really enjoyed taking part in the communal, musical numbers at the end of these Christmas shows. So far as Mylo was concerned, he had come to the finale of his latest performance and he was not going to disappoint his audience by leaving anything out!

With thespian flourish and the skill of a magician, Mylo produced a large, collapsible frame onto which a flip chart could be attached. He then spent some moments tripping over the frame, before fussing about how and where exactly he should put it up. He eventually settled on a spot almost exactly where he first showed it to everyone.

"Well, that took longer than I'd hoped," Mylo called out looking around at some animals to his right.

Everyone, including those animals, burst into giggles.

Mylo spun around and magically produced a flip chart, which he placed onto the frame. The frame promptly collapsed with a load clatter.

Everyone, except Mylo, started laughing loudly.

"You've all been messing with my stuff, haven't you?" demanded Mylo in mock annoyance.

"Oh no we haven't!" came the loud echoing reply from the warehouse's workforce .

"Oh yes you have!" bellowed Mylo in response.

"Oh no we haven't!" the warehouse thundered once more.

"Have it your way, then!" shouted Mylo in pretend exasperation.

Mylo managed to get the frame to stand up with the flip chart attached firmly to it.

A song was written upon the flip chart in clear bold writing.

Mylo flicked his right hand above his head. In an instant, he was baton twirling a very large wooden stick. He looked like an over-dressed school teacher in front of a class.

Mylo pointed his stick straight at Crocky, looked into his eyes and proclaimed, "My dear Clucky, you might be a little confused about what I'm doing?"

Crocky nodded slowly in response.

Mylo grinned and continued, "Come on everybody. We all know what happens now when we have a new starter. He needs our help remembering all of our acronyms. Come on. Get your singing voices ready. It's time for our Newbie Song!"

Cheers rang out everywhere. Crocky looked on a bit bemused.

Mylo turned towards Con and looked him up and down.

Mylo tutted and said, "And that includes you, Con. It might be nearly impossible for some to sing in tune, but please try your best."

That heralded even more guffaws. Con stuck out his tongue and pulled a silly face at Mylo in return.

Milo tutted again and sighed, "Charming! And to think we keep electing him as our union leader!"

That brought the house down with laughter, which crashed around the warehouse like joyous thunder.

Once more, Mylo spun around but this time in a mock-dramatic fashion. He pointed his stick at the first line of the song on the flip chart.

Mylo started, "Come along, everybody. We have a newbie, who needs to learn the ropes and the lingo. We all know this one. A one-two, a one, two, three, four:

The BB's the big engine, bringing EEs from middle Earth,

The HHs take the EEs to the CCs, their new berth,

We stack them high,

Into the sky,

Until the job is done,

Then the EEs go to RR, when she does her Easter Run!"

Mylo sang loudly. Some others joined in, but not very many and not very well. Mylo was not impressed.

"That was rubbish! I've heard better singing from my Great Aunt Maureen after she's had one too many glasses of sherry on Boxing Day!" chided Mylo.

He then created a competition to try to improve the singing.

Mylo said that everybody to his left were on Team One and everyone to his right were on Team Two. Whoever sang loudest would be declared the winner.

This competition did the trick. Both sides of the warehouse belted out the song. After lots of laughter and banter, Mylo declared the contest a draw. This was met with universal cheers, clapping and stamping of feet.

Mylo turned to Crocky and said softly, "My darling Clucky, it's as simple as that. Have fun. Working here is a joy!"

Mylo took out his pocket watch, studied it for a moment and exclaimed to everyone in a booming voice, "And look at the time. Luncheon awaits! Goodbye, farewell and *adieu*!"

With that Mylo bowed to Crocky, bowed to Con and then

bowed to the rest of his audience, before he waved, turned on his heals and left.

"Mylo really does like his pantos!" Crocky laughed to himself. "But it's lunch time. My tummy's been rumbling for ages. I must eat."

Con took Crocky to the nearest work's canteen, which was a few hundred yards in front of Warehouse C. It served everything imaginable and more. Crocky asked for Cornish Pasty and chips, followed by jelly and ice cream and all washed down with a large cup of orange juice. He received the lot – but also with an apple and a banana as the Easter Bunny was not going to let her staff just eat an unbalanced diet.

SN–cough, nom, nom, nom, the lunch disappeared very quickly into Crocky's tummy.

Con looked surprised. "My word, Clucky, you were hungry."

After lunch, Crocky started his work in earnest. He saw that the system was as brilliantly simple to operate in practice as in theory. He just had to keep alert. He found the job to be great fun with excellent camaraderie with his colleagues. Crocky discovered that the HH would even stop automatically for all breaks so he could never miss them. The HH also told him when his shift was over and it was time to go home. The HH would finish the day by parking itself in a charging bay so it would be ready for the next day's work.

At the end of the working day, the sides of the warehouses, where the goods trains had earlier stopped, were now full of passenger trains taking the staff home. The air was filled with small flashes and pop sounds as BB train after BB train came and went, teleporting everyone to their various places of abode in Easter Bunny Meadow's beautiful residential areas.

As Crocky stepped down from his HH, Con walked over to him.

Con asked, "Do you know where you will live down here, Clucky?"

It dawned upon Crocky that no one had told him anything about his living arrangements. He started to look a bit concerned.

Con noticed Crocky's change In mood and said, "Don't worry. Reception often forgets to tell newbies where they will go at the end of the day. The reason is probably because your mobile phone is programmed to take you to your new home, so they don't see the need. All you need to do is go to the side of the warehouse where everyone else is catching their BBs home, put your phone to your mouth and ask for a BB train to take you home. A BB will turn up, and the BB and your phone will take you there. Good luck. And remember, please be polite to the BB, unless you want to spend the night here! See you tomorrow."

Con gave Crocky a small wave and went off to catch a BB.

Chapter Twenty

Crocky's New Home

Crocky looked towards the sides of his warehouse. He could see queues of animals waiting for their turns to request BBs. At the head of those queues BBs would appear, animals would get into them, the BBs would disappear, new BBs would arrive and the process would start again.

Crocky walked to the end of the nearest queue and waited his turn. When he reached the front, he put his mobile phone to his mouth and remembered that the BB responded to politeness.

"Single creature passenger train to take me home, please," said Crocky clearly.

There was a small flash and a pop sound. Right in front of him appeared a single carriage train, which containing a single seat for him. The door to this BB was already open for Crocky.

Crocky stepped in, sat down and said, "Home, please."

The door closed gently and almost silently. There was another small flash and pop sound. Suddenly, Crocky noticed that the view outside his train had transformed from the warehouse zone to a residential area.

The door opened and Crocky stepped out. He was amazed

by the scale and beauty of this place. It would have been incredible on the surface of the Earth but this was hidden deep below the Devon countryside. As the train left with another small flash and pop, he saw that he was beside a most attractive, gently curving road, which had cherry and almond trees either side of it. Those trees were in their finest spring blossom colours of striking whites and every shade of pink one could possibly imagine. There was a gentle breeze, which caused some of this blossom to flutter to the floor like fresh confetti.

Crocky's phone spoke to him. It told him to look to his left and walk up a modestly sloping pathway. He followed his phone's advice and went up the footpath as it meandered between two hedges. These hedges were springing into vibrant green leaf beneath copious white and purple blossom.

After about fifty yards of this slight incline, he found a building that resembled a large manor house. His phone told him to go to the front door, push it and proceed to the first floor where his home was situated in Apartment 3.

As Crocky approached the front communal door to the building, his phone unlocked it for him automatically. He pushed it open and was given a choice of stairs or a bright and roomy lift. Crocky chose the lift. When he reached the first floor, his phone told him to turn right out of the elevator. Crocky did that and ahead of him he saw his new front door. He walked to his apartment and as he reached his front door he heard it unlocking for him through the magic of his mobile phone. He stepped into his new residence and was amazed by its size and quality.

His front door led to a hallway. Through a door to his left he had a living room with a large television mounted upon the wall, a sofa, a comfy chair, a coffee table and a sideboard.

The living room led to a kitchen. The kitchen had everything anyone could want, including a cooker, a double oven, a grill, a refrigerator, a freezer, a dishwasher, a larder cupboard, a sink and draining board, and a dining area with an oak table and four chairs. There was a utility room at the far side of this kitchen, which contained a combined washing machine with tumble drier and another sink.

Crocky noticed a leaflet in the middle of the dining table. That leaflet explained how everything in the kitchen and utility room worked. It emphasised that only requests which were reasonable, non-gluttonous and not greedy would be successful.

To get food and drink, all Crocky had to do was enter the kitchen and ask for whatever he wanted. He could ask for them to be cooked and prepared or to be uncooked and unprepared. He could ask for them to be put anywhere in kitchen or dining area, including being plated up and poured out for a meal.

After eating, if Crocky asked for the dishes and cutlery to be washed up and put away, the magic would do that for him.

If he had any clothing or linen that needed washing, drying or ironing, all he had to do was go to the utility room and ask for that to be done. Then the magic would sort it out.

Whenever he was in the kitchen or utility room, he could ask for his home, or anything in or on it, to be cleaned, repaired or replaced, and the magic would make sure it happened.

Crocky went back to his hallway and saw two doors to the right. One of those doors led to Crocky's bedroom. This contained a large double bed, a dressing table, a chest of drawers, a television mounted upon a wall and a wardrobe that went from the floor to the ceiling. Attached to his bedroom was a stylishly designed shower room with sink and toilet.

On his bed was another leaflet. It explained that when he was in his bedroom, if he wanted to move any items of clothing or linen, which were the utility room, all he had to do was ask for them to be put away anywhere in the house or be put on his bed and the magic would do the rest. The leaflet also said that if he wanted new clothing or linen, all he had to do was ask for those things in his bedroom. Those items would then appear on his bed. The leaflet stated in bold print that if the magic would not provide anything, it believed the requests to be unreasonable, gluttonous or greedy. The leaflet explained that there was no charge for the apartment, there were no energy or other bills to pay and all things and services which were provided by the magic were given to Clucky Diall free for so long as he worked for the Easter Bunny at Easter Bunny Meadow.

The second door on the right of the hallway opened into a bathroom, which contained a large bath of a corner spa design. This could produce huge numbers of bubbles in the water upon request. That bath also had an inbuilt set of lights within its enamel, which could be set to illuminate the water with the whole spectrum of colours in the rainbow.

Finally, Crocky's apartment had a large balcony, which overlooked a most picturesque riverside scene. In the distance, Crocky could see a horizon of glorious hills. Along the river's valley, on either side of the river, Crocky noticed numerous buildings. They had been made in a variety of designs and colours to augment and blend into the scenery. Everywhere there were flowers, trees, bushes, shrubs and grasses. The flora ranged from the most perfectly manicured lawns and topiary hedges to the beauty of apparently unkept, natural landscapes. It was a perfect example of how buildings and nature could be blended together to live and work in harmony.

"This is fantastic," Crocky told himself.

Crocky's phone beeped. He looked at it and saw that his phone was showing him a map of the locality, which included all kinds of amenities, shops, restaurants and other useful places.

Mary Mermicorn watched all of this and beamed to

herself. She thought her work with Crocky was now completed. His job meant that he would never come into contact with humans again. He would always get ample food and drink. His living and working conditions were permanent and fantastic. She could not believe that Crocky would ever want to leave this perfect and safe environment. She thought it was inconceivable that Crocky would now follow through with his thoughts of trying to steal lots of Easter chocolate from the Easter Bunny and jeopardise all of this wonderful life. She relaxed and stopped paying as much attention to what Crocky was doing or thinking as she had been doing. This was an significant error of judgment.

Chapter Twenty-One

Crocky's Plans Meet Slothful Security

Crocky loved his work. He loved where he lived. He loved the fact that he could get any food of any type he wanted. As long as he lived and worked in Easter Bunny Meadow, he knew that he would never have to eat any of the types of food that the animal park used to feed him.

However, he had managed to get this job by pretending to be a chicken without wings or tail feathers. He thought that he had to keep this pretence going forever. This meant he believed that he would have to keep wearing his costume permanently, whenever he was at work, outside or socialising. He was well aware that as spring moved into summer, even in England, the weather was going to get considerably warmer on many days. Due to his disguise being an almost all-enveloping coat of feathers with a bright orange piece of plastic around his face, Crocky knew that this attire was only going to become increasingly uncomfortable.

To add to Crocky's disenchantment, he thought that staying at Easter Bunny Meadow would condemn him to having to hide his true identity forever. He did not want to spend the rest of his life pretending to be a chicken.

Crocky did not realise that he could have gained employment with the Easter Bunny without the bother of any disguise. The Easter Bunny had employed a number of crocodiles around the world, particularly in Egypt and Australia. The Easter Bunny would not have turned away a small two-feet-long crocodile, who was escaping from humans.

Crocky had come to work at Easter Bunny Meadow alone. He remained very much by himself and did not make any real friends. This resulted in him spending a lot of time on his own. This allowed him many hours to think and contemplate. Having this large amount of reflective time started to make him feel sad and lonely rather quickly. Those feelings soon changed to ones of anger, bitterness and revenge.

He spent many hours ruminating about how humans had treated him and his family over his whole life. He resolved that he was going to pay them back by taking chocolate from the CCs because it was destined for human consumption. However, his plan was not just to take a small amount of chocolate. He had worked himself into such a furious frenzy of livid indignation, he decided that he would carry out the most punitive actions against humanity that he could. He would do this to compensate him for all of the distress and suffering people had caused him over the years. This meant that Crocky intended to eat all of the Easter eggs for England so that not a single human in that country would receive any chocolate on Easter morning.

Every evening, Crocky would lie down on his extremely comfy bed. He would smile an evil, vengeful smile. He would let his teeth show and glint in his bedroom's lights under his beak disguise.

Crocky would mutter to himself, "You humans have done so much to me without any consequences... Until NOW! *SNAP!*"

His heart and his head had become filled with all-encompassing, irrational and unfair anger and negativity against all humans. The problem with such all-consuming emotions is that they can remove the ability to see the good from the bad, or to ensure that blame and responsibility are apportioned to the right people. This can result in wrong choices being made, including forgetting that just because some humans do bad things, it does not mean that every human is responsible for that naughtiness!

Crocky stopped believing that he should never allow himself to punish the innocent and guilty alike for the bad deeds of the guilty alone. Justice is rightful: revenge is wrongful. Crocky lost his understanding of that concept. In spite of his really good situation, Crocky let his desire for payback against humanity, plus his greedy tummy, get the better of him.

Over the next few weeks, Crocky observed everything within Easter Bunny Meadow with keen interest, attention to detail and copious eavesdropping upon conversations. Crocky thought he had discovered all that he needed to know to pull off his great chocolate theft. He knew that the amount of chocolate he intended to take was so vast he would only get one shot at it. No one could hide stealing all of England's Easter eggs for long.

Crocky knew that the Easter Bunny was a very fair and caring employer. She had even banned overtime or night-time working on the basis that no one should be worked too hard and everyone should be properly rested. This prohibition had one exception: the night before Easter Day itself.

However, the Easter Bunny rewarded her colleagues for this one-night shift per year by giving them the rest of Easter Sunday off as soon as all of the Easter eggs had been delivered. She then let them all have all of Easter Monday off work as well. This became their big party day. Finally, she let them have all of the next day off too so that her staff had a day to recover from the excesses of Easter Monday's celebrations and partying!

Crocky could have decided to carry on working and enjoy celebrating and eating as much as he liked after the Easter Bunny had delivered all of her eggs, but he chose not to do that. Indeed, rather than appreciating and respecting the Easter Bunny's kind heart and generous nature, Crocky regarded those positive character traits as weaknesses to be exploited for his plans.

Crocky knew that the Easter Bunny ran her business based upon trust. He had checked, and checked again many times, but he was not aware of any CCTV cameras, alarm systems or security guards. He had heard that no one had ever tried to steal or be really naughty in any of the Easter Bunny's premises, and so she did not believe that anyone would.

The only issue at the Devon site of which he was aware involved Grandeur Fox. Crocky had heard all about that because that episode had entered into the folklore of Easter Bunny Meadow. It was the postscript to the incident which raised Crocky's attention the most, though. He was told that following those events, Chomper had tried to persuade the Easter Bunny and Prudence to install CCTV and alarm systems all over the site, but they had declined to do so.

After much scheming, Crocky concluded that the optimum time to strike was the night before Palm Sunday, which was when the warehouses reached their points of 'Maximum Chocolate'. The last Easter Egg deliveries into the warehouses would arrive on that Saturday. Thereafter, the chocolate would start getting moved into their positions for rapid transferring to the Easter Bunny on Easter night. Palm Sunday that year also happened to be Crocky's birthday. In his troubled mind, Crocky began to believe that fate had decreed that he should destroy all of the humans' Easter eggs on the day before his birthday, just like humans had destroyed his family and his life on the day before his birthday all those years ago.

Crocky's plan had one flaw. His knowledge of Easter Bunny Meadow's security arrangements was not completely accurate.

Crocky was totally unaware that once Chomper's suggestions about installing CCTV and alarm systems were turned down, she did not give up. Chomper responded to this rejection by researching all relevant health and safety regulations. Yes, magical places have to comply with various magical realms' health and safety rules just like so many Earthly countries and regions.

Armed with that official information, Chomper wrote a detailed report about where she believed Easter Bunny Meadow's security procedures fell afoul of those rules. Chomper's tenacious perseverance did produce a result, but not the one Chomper or anyone could have expected.

When they received Chomper's health and safety submissions, the Easter Bunny and Prudence thanked her for her hard work and said that they would consider what she had written. In truth, they did not really want to do anything because they had so much faith in animal nature. Their views were that their chocolate operations were purely based on love, kindness, respect and wholly non-threatening behaviours. They believed that this meant that no one would ever think of being deliberately unpleasant at Easter Bunny Meadow. Therefore, they considered that any extra security measures were not needed and would never be required. It was in this frame of mind that they read Chomper's report and scrutinised the relevant health and safety rules in detail.

After about half an hour, the Easter Bunny and Prudence looked up at each other in surprise. Chomper had found some new regulations, which were going to come into force in only fifteen days' time. Those regulations meant that some additional security was going to be needed. However, the

Easter Bunny was given a wide discretion about what new measures she had to put in place. These new rules certainly did not specify that CCTV or alarm systems had to be installed.

The Easter Bunny and Prudence sighed in unison at the discovery of these additional requirements. They started discussing what would be the least intrusive measures that they could put in place to satisfy any health and safety inspector, who might come along. They were having a hard time coming up with a plan, in part because they disagreed with what the new regulations said, even though they knew that they had to comply with them.

In an effort to stimulate their brain cells, Prudence decided to make a pot of tea. She put a couple of tea bags into a teapot, which was made out of extremely strong clear glass. She walked over to a hot water dispenser, filled up the pot and placed it onto the conference table upon which they were working. She returned to her chair and sat down. The room was filled with silence as the Easter Bunny and Prudence stared at the brown English Breakfast tea slowly diffusing through the nearly boiling water, hoping to find any inspiration from that process. The quiet was then abruptly broken by the Easter Bunny's phone.

She answered it. It was an emergency.

At the same time as the Easter Bunny and Prudence were contemplating health and safety matters, two sloths were being transported by van between zoos. Their route took them over the beautiful Mendip Hills in Somerset.

During their journey, the weather took a distinct turn for the worse. Torrential rain and hill fog had reduced visibility to a few yards only. As the van's driver tried to deal with these really bad weather conditions, he became hopelessly lost high up above Cheddar Gorge. He decided that he needed to get off the hilltops and hope the conditions improved lower down. This meant driving down a very windy and steep road, which had been transformed by the deluge into a ranging torrent full of torn out vegetation and dislodged stones. The poor driver had no chance of seeing the submerged rock that had been washed onto the carriageway ahead of him. There was an almighty bang. The van flipped over. Its back doors burst open. The cages in which the sloths were being housed were flung out into the elements.

The two sloths were adorably cute, predominantly brown creatures. Their names were Harry and Sophie Sloth. They were siblings. Harry was a few years older than his sister. Neither of them had a clue what was going on. They had both been awoken by the bang. Then their worlds were literally turned upside down, and round and round.

Their cages bounced down the craggy hillside for a couple of hundred yards. Within half a second of one another, their cages' doors broke open and the two shocked sloths were jettisoned out of their captivity. These animals were catapulted along a hard and uneven declivity for a few dozen more feet, before they shot across a coarse, grassy slope and fell into a narrow rocky crevice. The sloths were left confused, dazed and wet. They could not get out, so they did what sloths do best: nothing. They huddled together, hoped for rescue and snoozed.

Their cages were now just horribly twisted pieces of metalwork. They had continued to career down the hillside before coming to rest about four hundred yards away from the sloths' limestone enclosure.

When the human rescue team arrived, the weather was still appalling. They managed to save the driver. He was taken to a local hospital, where he was treated for a broken right arm and a large number of cuts and bruises, which were dotted all over him. Thankfully, in due course, he made a full recovery.

His van was not so fortunate. The rescuers managed to lift the battered vehicle onto the back of a flatbed truck and take it very carefully into a garage at Cheddar. The garage owner took one look at its mangled shape, breathed in and out slowly and loudly, shook his head and gently rubbed his stubbly chin. The van was irreparable. The garage took the destroyed vehicle. It was able to break it down, recycle and re-use some of it as spare parts, before sending the remainder of the van to a local scrap yard.

The rescuers, though, could not find the sloths. They saw their destroyed cages, which led them to search in completely the wrong part of the hillside. They eventually came to the sad, sodden and very cold conclusion that the sloths must have been killed in the crash. The weather was too bad for the rescuers to continue their search, and so they reluctantly left the scene. Despondently, they left the hillside fearing that the sloths would end up being taken away by a fox or some other carnivores for their dinner.

Whilst it certainly did not seem like it to them at that moment, Harry and Sophie Sloth were in luck. The Mendip Hills are home to lots of wildlife. Some of their most famous residents are the mountain goats. Mandy Mountain-Goat was munching vegetation in the driving rain about twenty feet away from where the van had overturned. At the exact moment of this crash, the swirling hill fog had cleared just enough where Mandy was standing to enable her to see the sloths flying out of the van and where they ended up.

Mandy had lived in those hills for many years, so she knew every nook and cranny. Furthermore, she was highly experienced in being able to walk up and down those hills to find exact spots, even when she could not see due to low cloud. Therefore, when the fog closed in around her again, she was easily able to trot around the crash site. She knew some humans would turn up to deal with the aftermath quite quickly. She walked slowly to a position quite close to the van's resting place and waited. Sure enough, within ten minutes rescuers had arrived. Mandy watched their work, whilst chewing on some particularly tasty wild thyme. She was impressed by how they saved the driver. She admired how they recovered the van. So far as their efforts to find the sloths were concerned, Mandy thought that their forlorn attempts were rather amusing.

Once she was sure that the humans had left the scene, Mandy wandered over to the crevice.

"Hi, I'm Mandy. How are you two doing down there?" asked Mandy brightly.

She positioned herself over the narrow hole in the rocks to stop some of the rain falling onto the trapped sloths.

The sloths slowly woke up and opened their eyes. They spoke together in a steady, ponderous manner, "Hi. We're Harry and Sophie Sloth. We're all right, but we're stuck. Can you help, please?"

Mandy replied, "Of course. I'll just make a quick phone call and you'll be out really soon."

Harry and Sophie looked at each other. They had not seen a goat with a phone before. In fact, they had not seen any animals with phones before, except for humans. They were rather taken aback.

Mandy had this phone because she was a West Country Ambassador for Easter Bunny Meadow. Her role was to find suitable new recruits for that site. Her phone was linked directly to the recruitment department. As Mandy made her call, the recruitment department was having a short team meeting. The Easter Bunny had volunteered to look after any incoming calls whilst the meeting took place. She liked keeping involved in a hands-on way (or should that be a paws-on way?) covering as many aspects of her business as possible. As a result, Mandy's call went straight to the phone in the Easter Bunny's office, just as the Easter Bunny and Prudence were trying to work out how to respond to Chomper's health and safety points. Mandy was stunned when she realised that her call was answered by the Easter Bunny herself.

As Mandy explained the sloths' predicament, the Easter Bunny put her phone on loud speaker so Prudence could hear as well. As they listened to Mandy, they continued to stare at the continuing tea currents in their transparent teapot. Suddenly, at virtually the same time, they had an idea. This was not an unusual occurrence for these best friends. They had worked together for so long, it often seemed as if their brains worked like linked super-computers. They smiled at each other and nodded. The juxtaposition of slow-moving brown sloths and slow-moving brown tea currents had presented them with an unexpected plan.

They agreed with Mandy that the sloths needed rescuing and could do a job at Easter Bunny Meadow. Within moments, the Easter Bunny had dispatched Easter Bunny Meadow's most experienced St Bernard rescue dog and her team of four puppies to the gorge. They soon met up with Mandy and rescued Harry and Sophie. Once the sloths had thanked Mandy many times over, the rescuers teleported Harry and Sophie to Easter Bunny Meadow. Once there, the site's medical teams took care of them. They were a bit bumped and bruised, and somewhat cold and wet, but amazingly they had suffered no other injuries. They were soon patched up and provided with warm, dry clothing. They were placed into adjoining hospital beds for rest and recuperation, plus lots of food and drink.

When Harry and Sophie were settled and comfortable, the Easter Bunny and Prudence came to visit them. After checking that they were going to be all right and that they were being cared for well, they offered Harry and Sophie jobs.

Harry and Sophie were given the opportunity to work and live together for as long as they liked in Easter Bunny Meadow. They were asked to become the security guards at the warehouses. Prudence pointed out to the sloths that there was a complete lack of crime within the warehouses – or anywhere else within Easter Bunny Meadow for that matter. The Easter Bunny explained that they could spend as much time as they liked hanging upside from anything in or around the warehouses. The Easter Bunny continued that because there was no crime, there would be nothing for them to do other than be in the warehouse area where they could sleep, rest, eat and drink to their hearts' content. She also told them that because there was zero crime, it did not matter even if they fell asleep on the job.

The Easter Bunny and Prudence finished their recruitment pitch to the Sloth siblings telling them that they really wanted to work with them but they would understand and respect fully any decision that they made to the contrary. However, they had to make Harry and Sophie aware that if they declined these jobs, they could not stay at Easter Bunny Meadow once they had recovered. That would mean it would be highly likely that they would soon get found by some humans and sent back to a zoo. Harry and Sophie did not fancy the zoo option. They were immediately appointed as the security guards.

Once they had recovered from their injuries, Harry and Sophie fit into their new roles really quickly. They were well-liked by the relatively small number of animals, who came across them, because they were never any bother to anyone, whether they were asleep or awake. They spent most of their time hanging upside down in the quietest spots so they were never in the way. On the relatively few occasions anyone found them to be awake, they were always very pleasant. Of course, they never caught any suspects or criminals because no one ever did anything wrong.

After these successful appointments, the Easter Bunny spoke with Chomper. She thanked Chomper for raising such important health and safety issues. She told Chomper about the decision to appoint Harry and Sophie Sloth as the security guards rather than get CCTV and alarm systems.

Chomper was pleased that her points had been taken seriously. However, she was confused by how they had been resolved.

She asked the Easter Bunny, "How can sloths be the security guards and comply with the new health and safety rules?"

The Easter Bunny replied with a grin, and a twinkle in her eyes, which could almost have been described as slightly mischievous had she not been the Easter Bunny, "These new health and safety rules say that we have to have security measures on site to deal with external or internal threats."

The Easter Bunny paused for a moment to check Chomper's reaction. Chomper was smiling and nodding in agreement so that was fine.

The Easter Bunny continued, "We do not have to add anything to deal with any potential external threats because our site is completely underground with instantly sealable entrances and exits, and it has its invisibility shield. However, I agree that under these new rules, we need to create some specific security measures for internal threats. So we had to ask ourselves, what are the internal threats to Easter Bunny Meadow?"

The Easter Bunny paused and gave Chomper a quizzical look.

Chomper felt like she had to give some reply, so she said, "Well, err... I can't think of any off the top of my head."

"You're quite right, Chomper," responded the Easter Bunny. "There aren't any. But the new rules say we have to have security measures to protect us from internal threats with no exceptions. Clearly they had no idea about our unique site here when they came up with these new laws. Nevertheless, we have no choice but to comply with them."

She gave a sigh and then said, "The rules do help us a bit because they say that we should only put in place security measures to the extent necessary, appropriate and proportionate to safeguard each unique workplace, taking into account the level and nature of the threats and that workplace's particular circumstances. So if Easter Bunny Meadow was overrun with widespread naughtiness – which I must state categorically it is NOT! – then I would be rushing to create comprehensive CCTV, alarm and internal policing systems for our health and safety, which the rules would allow and require."

"Yes, that makes sense," interjected Chomper.

"But we have no internal threats here. The rules require me to put in place necessary, appropriate and proportionate security measures to deal with our particular internal threats, which are ZERO! The rules ban me from implementing more stringent and intrusive measures that are not commensurate with the level of internal threats. Therefore, I had to come up with internal security arrangements to deal with non-existent threats. The answer was appointing sloths as the security guards. If you think about it, Chomper, who can possibly claim that sloths are not qualified to do jobs protecting us from ZERO internal threats?" concluded the Easter Bunny raising and twisting her front right paw in an extravagant flourish.

Chomper considered this answer for a few seconds and

then laughed. "I can't argue with that logic."

The Easter Bunny was pleased. They said their farewells and departed each other's company on very good terms, as always.

Everyone was happy. Chomper had raised concerns and they had been properly considered and action taken.

Harry and Sophie had recovered, they were no longer in captivity and they had jobs, which they loved and were everything that had been promised to them. As expected, Harry and Sophie did not really do anything, except one vital, legally required thing. They enabled the Easter Bunny to tick a new mandatory box on the health and safety inspector's latest checklist. That made the Easter Bunny and Prudence happy too.

Of course, the nature of the work, or lack of it, carried out by Harry and Sophie led to no one ever remembering to mention them to Crocky, so he was oblivious to their existence.

Chapter Twenty-Two

Crocky's Slothful Discovery

The day before Palm Sunday was lovely. The sun shone brightly; its rays showering the dew-laden grasses with sparkling jewels. The daffodils nodded rhythmically in gentle waves in the light southerly breeze, as if dancing with nature. Crocky, though, paid not a jot of attention to this. His completely undivided focus was on that evening.

He went to work as usual. The only slight change to his daily routine was that he did not eat any breakfast or lunch. Whilst he was aware that he had the ability to eat ridiculously huge amounts of human food without ever getting full or suffering any ill-effects, he thought it would not hurt to leave a bit of extra tummy space for the chocolate he was going to devour later on that day.

When Crocky completed his shift in the late afternoon, he started to execute his plan. As everyone else was taking their BBs home, Crocky snuck back into Warehouse C and hid. He went right into the middle of the warehouse and climbed up four CCs. He lay as flat as he could, whilst still being just about able to watch and check that everybody went home.

Yum, yum, yum, he thought. *Not long now. I can almost taste the chocolate already.*

He licked his lips in anticipation.

Crocky watched the last workers leave. He lay still. He waited. He wanted to make absolutely sure that he had not missed a single animal or that someone did not return to retrieve a forgotten coat, for instance.

As he lay in the absolute silence of the warehouse, his thoughts once again turned to how humans had mistreated him and his family over the years, and how he was completely justified in what he was going to do. Like many who seek revenge, Crocky was still mentally trying to concoct explanations and reasons for completely unacceptable behaviour.

At just past 23.00, Crocky was sure he was alone and the coast was clear. He inched his way out of his hiding position, made one last check all around him and then smiled a huge, malevolent grin. His time had come. His time for payback!

In a blur of speed and energy, Crocky sprung into life. The noise and intensity of his actions were incredible. There was an incessant, echoing and rolling cacophony of sounds. Not only was there the almost constant thunder of "*SNAP*" and "*NOM, NOM, NOM*", the air was also filled with the harsh tones of Easter eggs' packaging been torn apart, and with Crocky scrambling and crashing between CCs as he charged around the warehouse stuffing every last piece of chocolate into his mouth. When he had eaten the contents of Warehouse C, he just shot off into another warehouse and carried on. Incredibly, as Crocky progressed from warehouse to warehouse, he seemed to be increasing his speed of chocolate demolition.

As he devoured, Crocky built himself up into an ever-increasing rage of selfish self-pity and self-justification. These powerful and destructive feelings exploded as the clock turned the day into Palm Sunday – Crocky's birthday. This had the effect of amplifying Crocky's fury about what had happened to him and his family on that dreadful birthday all those years ago.

Crocky kept silently saying to himself over and over again, "This will teach all you humans for being horrible to me, to my family and to so many other animals for so long. This will teach you for stopping my Christmas treats. Your children will wake up on Easter morning and get what you truly deserve – NOTHING! This is why the mermaid princess gave me these powers; to avenge the greed and horridness of humanity!"

In truth, Crocky was not eating all of England's Easter eggs for any altruistic or helpful motive for anyone else. He was not getting justice for anybody. None of the chocolate he was consuming was supposed to be going to anyone who had done anything wrong to him, his family or any animals. The Easter Bunny does not give Easter eggs to naughty people. In Crocky's greedy rage, he was punishing the innocent.

Crocky carried on through the night. As the sun's first light was starting to shine on Palm Sunday morning, Crocky entered the last warehouse. This huge building was a spectacular representation of Powderham Castle. Crocky was oblivious to its architectural brilliance. He zoomed inside to continue his feeding frenzy into his bottomless pit of a tummy. He was loving every scrummy moment of it. He was even starting to feel a smug sense of pride at how cleverly he was carrying out his plan.

Then it was over. Crocky reached and ate England's last Easter Egg, which was at the bottom of a CC right at the back of this warehouse. He finished swallowing the last tasty piece of chocolate and threw his head back in pleasure. He roared out a huge cheer. He started to wonder if there was any way he could take the BB to the Florida site. After all, that was five hours behind UK time so he would have plenty of time in which to eat all of their chocolate before daybreak. Then he thought he could pop over to the Hawaii site and do the same there. He started licking his lips again.

These thoughts to take his greedy revenge to the USA were the start of Crocky's downfall. The third reasonable clarification of the mermaid princess's spell allowed Mary Mermicorn to warn any appropriate humans or animals to stop Crocky if he started using the spell in completely unacceptable ways. If Crocky managed to get away with eating all of England's Easter chocolate, it was clear that he was not going to stop there or anywhere for that matter. This meant that his behaviour had moved from merely unacceptable to completely unacceptable in the eyes of the spell, which resulted in the spell sending a magical warning signal straight to Mary Mermicorn.

As it was the early hours of the morning, Mary was asleep.

"COMPLETELY UNACCEPTABLE BEHAVIOUR!" blasted out the magical alarm into both of Mary's ears.

Mary awoke with a start. Her room was filled with a flashing red light and the audible warning was being repeated again and again.

She realised immediately that Crocky must have overstepped the mark. She ordered the alarms to stop, which they did, and used her magic to look at what Crocky was doing. Her heart sank. Mary knew that Crocky had blown his chance at Easter Bunny Meadow. She had to prevent Crocky from continuing his chocolate thieving, but the third reasonable clarification meant that she was only allowed to stop him indirectly. She had to get humans or animals to intervene to prevent any continuation of his naughtiness. Crocky, though, appeared to be in a completely empty warehouse zone with no humans or animals anywhere near him.

Mary groaned at that thought. In desperation, she searched the warehouses for signs of other creatures. To her astonishment, she found Harry and Sophie Sloth. Most fortuitously, they were in the same warehouse where Crocky had finished munching. They were hanging upside down in a dark and shadowy corner, within clear sight of Crocky – or they would have been in clear sight of him had they not been fast asleep as usual. Crocky had not spotted their existence at all.

Mary sent herself into the sloths' dreams and shouted,

"WAKE UP!"

That did not work.

Mary used her magic to start shaking them as well as shouting at them in their dreams.

That did not work.

Then a mischievous idea came into Mary's mind. Whilst Mary remained in their dreams, she picked up a very large jug, which was full of a gallon of water.

Then she told both sloths very loudly, "I think we all need to go to the toilet!"

As she was saying those words, Mary proceeded to pour the contents of the jug very slowly, very loudly and most deliberately into a toilet that she had just conjured up in their dreams. The juxtaposition of these factors had an almost instant physical affect upon the sloths. They woke up at once feeling extremely uncomfortable and in need of the bathroom! Crocky just happened to be looking in their direction as two sets of desperate looking eyes peered straight at him as if they were suspended in the air.

"HELP! GHOSTS!" screamed Crocky, thinking he had awoken a terrifyingly horrible apparition.

Harry and Sophie Sloth may not have been the quickest or

the most wide-awake members of staff, but they knew a thief when they saw one.

"STOP, THIEF!" they shouted together, momentarily forgetting that they needed the toilet.

"*ARGH! SNAP!* A four-eyed, ghoulish security guard!" shouted Crocky in utter panic. "Oh no! I resign! I need to leave now!"

Crocky immediately summoned a BB to take him to the reception. Whilst he knew that Easter Bunny magic could not be used for naughtiness, Crocky hoped that this prohibition would not be a problem. He thought that the BB would have transported him out of the site if he had been sacked for stealing chocolate, so surely it would also take a resigning worker away from Easter Bunny Meadow to save the Easter Bunny the time and money of a formal disciplinary hearing to sack him!

Crocky called this correctly; much to his relief. With a small flash and a pop a small train arrived to take him out of there to the reception. He flung himself into the open BB.

"Reception, please, *SNAP!*" blurted out Crocky really quickly, remembering that he had to be polite. After another pop and a flash, he saw that he was at the reception.

By now the sloths had alerted everyone about what was happening. They were also making their way, as fast as sloths could, to get to the bathroom to relieve their discomfort!

A large group of very angry animals flooded towards the reception to try to capture Crocky.

Crocky burst out of his BB. In the distance, he could hear an approaching crowd of very upset animals. He was not going to hang around to see if he could apologise and make amends. He raced towards the exit. He had never run so fast in his life.

"Open exit, PLEASE!" he bellowed at the exit door, which obliged his desperate request.

As he shot out of the door, he suddenly noticed that his chicken disguise was disintegrating around him. Feathers were flying out of his crocodile skin jacket in all directions. His traffic cone beak was flapping wildly again at the top of his nose. Crocky could not understand why this was happening as he headed away from Easter Bunny Meadow as fast as his legs could carry him. The reality was that his disguise only worked because of Mary's magic. Her spell allowed it to remain and no one to spot that he was not a real chicken, so long as he was trying to get a job at Easter Bunny Meadow or actually working there. As soon as Crocky said he resigned, the spell was cancelled. This meant that Harry and Sophie Sloth were the first animals in Easter Bunny Meadow to see that he was really a crocodile in a chicken costume. When they raised the alarm, they warned everybody accordingly.

The crowd of chasing animals, including the Easter Bunny,

were gaining on Crocky and he ran away. By now he could make out a number of their shouts. Many were demanding that he stop and come back.

SNAP. No chance! SNAP, he thought to himself. *Do they think I'm completely stupid?*

He kept sprinting in a straight-line and saw the River Otter ahead. The bend of the river meant that he had only two options: surrender or swim. The head of the chasing pack was only about six feet behind him as he reached the river bank. By this time, he was snapping and shrieking in panic. He felt that he had no alternative. He took the longest leap he had ever taken in his whole life and he flung himself into the river.

"SPLASH!"

Crocky hit the water with a huge belly flop. Water sprayed up from the river in a massive fountain. Crocodiles can usually swim. Sadly for Crocky, he was trying to swim whilst wearing a tatty, now waterlogged and very heavy, feather jacket. He had also been winded heavily by the inelegant way in which his body had crashed into the cold currents. Moreover, he was panicking about being caught for single-handedly wiping out all of the Easter eggs and other Easter chocolate for England. This meant that on this occasion, he could not swim. Crocky felt himself sinking to the bottom of the River Otter. The animals on the bank just saw him sink without a trace.

This is it for me! thought Crocky as he hit the pebbled river floor. Suddenly and inexplicably, his panic left him. He felt strangely relaxed and relieved. In his mind, he called out to his mother. He then saw in his dreams his mother's loving and smiling face, which moved towards him and gave him a kiss. His dreams then stopped.

The Easter Bunny and everybody on the river bank decided that Crocky had drowned. The Easter Bunny and Prudence were very upset about this. They did not wish anyone to be hurt, regardless of what they might have done. Upon reflection, over the next few hours and days, many of the other workers at Easter Bunny Meadow felt similarly sad.

Mary Mermicorn had seen Crocky falling to the bottom of the River Otter and felt helpless. She was only tasked to save Crocky from humans. The magic did not include allowing her to save Crocky from angry animals so there was nothing she could do. She closed her eyes and a few tears began to roll down her cheeks. In spite of Crocky's naughtiness, there was something loveable about him.

"What a terrible shame," murmured Mary to herself.

Chapter Twenty-Three

Crocky's Salvation

Many of the best deeds are those selfless acts carried out to help or save others. They are never done for any reward. They are done purely because they are the right things to do. Over the whole world, selfless acts are performed, almost invariably without fanfare and with little or no recognition, but they keep on happening. It is a wonder of nature.

Occasionally, a selfless action can lead to amazing and unexpected things happening. In spite of all of his naughtiness, Crocky's heart and soul were not completely made of stone. Deep down, he still knew the difference between right and wrong, and between kindness and unpleasantness. In certain instances, Crocky's better nature could still shine through. The Trout family could attest to that.

The Trout family had been swimming in the river at its closest point to Easter Bunny Meadow when they heard some shouting on land. As they were in the water, they had no idea what this was about. So far as the Trout family was concerned, it was none of their business. They were just having a pleasant and leisurely family swim, whilst some land dwellers were being a bit rowdy.

However, the noise became really loud very quickly. Mr Trout popped his head out of the water to see what all the cacophony was about. Just as he did this, he saw Crocky launching himself through the air from the riverbank.

In that split second, Mr Trout noticed two things. Firstly, he noticed Crocky's attire. Mr Trout thought it was some kind of peculiar fancy dress costume, which was really poorly made due to the large number of bits flying off it. Secondly, he saw the front of the chasing group, which was making all that racket.

Mr Trout had no time to acquaint himself of anything else because gravity intervened. Crocky struck the water surface about six inches away from Mr Trout. There was such a large splash that its force knocked Mr Trout towards the riverbed. As Mr Trout recovered his equilibrium, he saw Crocky struggling.

Mrs Trout, Tina and Tiny had felt the splash but fortunately for them they were just far enough away that they were not caught up in Crocky's down current. They all turned and saw what was happening.

The whole Trout family swam towards Crocky as fast as their fins and tails could carry them. They saw him hit the stones on the riverbed. As they reached Crocky, they noticed that he had stopped struggling. He looked peaceful. His eyes were closed. He appeared like he had just fallen asleep. They knew that they did not have long to save him.

Mrs Trout noticed a large, metal, old-fashioned, upturned bath, which had jammed into the riverbank about twelve feet away from them. It had been washed down the river by the storms.

"Quick!" shouted Mrs Trout to her family. "Get Crocky into that tub. I'm sure there's an air pocket in there!"

Tina and Tiny looked at Mrs Trout in astonishment thinking, *How does Mummy know that?*

Mr Trout saw his children's expressions, but he trusted his wife completely.

He shouted to their children, "Mummy's clever and knows loads of stuff! Let's get him in there!"

Mrs Trout knew that there was an air pocket in the bath because her good friend Mrs Frog had told her about it a few days earlier. Mrs Frog was an inquisitive animal. Many in the river would even describe her as being a bit nosey. She could not resist going inside the newly arrived bathtub to have a look. She was so excited to find an air pocket in it that she could not wait to tell all of her friends, which she did, many times over.

Two things kept Crocky alive. Firstly, it was his size. The four trout could never have managed to move a full-size crocodile. Further, such a large creature could never have fit inside the bathtub. However, Crocky's small stature, together with partial water buoyancy, river currents flowing towards the bath, and a gap between the rim of the upturned bath and the riverbed immediately below it, which was just large enough for Crocky to squeeze through, gave the four trout the chance to push and half-float him to safety.

Secondly, it was his selfless acts of help and protection towards the Trout family a few weeks earlier. The whole Trout family did not just appreciate him for them, they loved him. It was a permanent, deeply emotional and unconditional love. It was the type of love that can give anyone more strength than they thought possible. They were not going to let the creature, who had saved Tiny and Tina, and who had warned the whole family of the dangers of the newly repaired dam, perish at the bottom of the river without a fight. With the strength of sharks, and the perseverance of salmon, they moved, bounced and squeezed Crocky into the bath. Mrs Trout just hoped that nothing had gone wrong since Mrs Frog's visited to have destroyed the air pocket.

The Trout family followed Crocky into the bath. To their joy and relief, there was still a large air pocket within it. Crocky floated to the water's surface. His head came to rest on the inner side of the bath with his mouth just out of the water.

The Trouts started to stroke Crocky. They were praying and willing that he would wake up and be all right. Suddenly, he coughed very loudly, spluttered out a lot of water, and his eyes opened wide.

It was very dark inside the tub. Crocky was confused with no idea where he was. Mr Trout shot out of the bath and rushed to Electra Eel's home within some nearby reeds. He asked her to come over and use her electrical prowess to provide some light in the bath. She readily agreed and hurried back with Mr Trout. Once inside the metal container, she lit her electric blue light. That instantly reflected around the bath's still shiny sides providing a good amount of illumination.

Crocky could now see his surroundings but he could not fathom out where he was or what was going on. He did, though, see the anxious faces of the Trout family around him. He started to remember falling into the river and began to work out what must have happened. He burst into tears.

"Thank you. *SNAP*. Words fail me!" sobbed Crocky.

The Trout family burst into tears too. Joy and relief filled the bath.

"Why did you save me?" asked Crocky.

"Because we love you and you saved my brother," replied Tina.

The whole Trout family then joined together, "Yes, we love you, Crocky. You will always be part of our family. We will always look out for you."

For the first time since he was orphaned, Crocky felt the true and unconditional love of a family. He was completely overcome with emotion and started to feel faint. Then all the Trout family moved over to his head and kissed him together. That finished the job.

CLUNK! went Crocky as he lost consciousness and slid down the inside of the bath.

The Trout family looked aghast. Fortunately, Crocky's face went into the cold water and that shock woke him up again. The Trouts decided that it was probably not a wise thing to kiss him again. It was far too dangerous!

The Trouts explained to Crocky where he was. Crocky thanked them again. He paused to consider his situation. He thought the air pocket was pretty big so he decided that staying where he was for a little while longer, whilst things calmed down in and around Easter Bunny Meadow, would be a very good idea.

"Could you help me out of this feather jacket, please?" Crocky asked the Trout family.

"Of course," they all replied, before almost immediately regretting it. It was certainly not the easiest of tasks to try to peel off a waterlogged, feathery, crocodile skin jacket that covered nearly all of Crocky in the confined space of an upturned bath. There were lots of "ouches", "mind outs" and exasperated sighing before Crocky was free from that garment.

"We'll take it to the Swans upstream," said Mr Trout. "They will be able to dry it out and use it for nesting. They're so big and their children are always so boisterous, their nest is always in need of repairs."

"If you are all right here, we will leave you and let you have a rest. Do you still need Electra with her light?" asked Mrs Trout kindly.

Crocky smiled an exhausted smile. "No, that's fine. I'd like a little sleep. All I would ask would be for updates as to what is going on at Easter Bunny Meadow, if that is all right please? I think it would be sensible to make sure that the coast is clear up there before I pop out! Thank you, Electra, and thank you, my dear Trout family."

The Trouts started to leave, followed by Electra Eel.

Just as they waved goodbye, Tiny Trout turned and asked Crocky, "Why were you wearing all those feathers?"

Crocky thought for a second.

"*SNAP*. I was cold and we all know feathers keep birds warm, so I thought I'd try them out," he lied. "You never know stuff until you try, eh? Chicken feathers are great until you get them wet. Then they get too soggy, they weigh you down and they make you even colder. I've decided that scales are much better than feathers? Wouldn't you and your sister agree?"

"Oh yes, scales are much better than feathers!" shouted Tina and Tiny giggling.

The Trout family and Electra then left Crocky, who closed

his eyes for a sleep.

Mary Mermicorn had watched the Trout family save Crocky in awe and amazement in equal measure. She smiled. She would still have the mermaid princess's magic to carry out for a while longer.

The Trouts swam up the river and handed the feather jacket to a very grateful Mr and Mrs Swan, who were yet again trying to fix their nest, thanks to their six cheeky and destructive cygnets.

The Swan parents told the Trout family about all the excitement they had noticed at Easter Bunny Meadow, including the arrival of some of Santa's elves. The Swans commented that they were pleased it was all quiet there now because their cygnets went from being really scared with all of the shouting to exuberant over-excitement when they saw the elves; hence the damaged nest!

After they had finished their chat, Mrs Trout went home with Tina and Tiny. Mr Trout, though, took a detour home. He swam rapidly back to the bath, where Crocky was not quite asleep.

As it was completely dark inside the tub, Mr Trout called out to let Crocky know he was coming in. He apologised for disturbing Crocky, but he explained that he called out because he did not want to scare him.

"Crocky, as you asked, I have an update for you about Easter Bunny Meadow," said Mr Trout.

"Thank you. What is it?" asked Crocky, stifling a tired yawn.

Mr Trout explained, "Easter Bunny Meadow is now all quiet but some of Santa's elves have turned up there. I have no idea why. We've never seen any of Santa's workforce around here before, so something important must be happening. If we find out anything more, we'll let you know. Anyway, I'd better get back home now and let you get your rest. Bye, Crocky."

"Bye. Safe journey home," called Crocky, as he heard Mr Trout swimming away.

Crocky settled down to sleep, thinking about this news. As he drifted to sleep, a mischievous grin spread across his face. Mary Mermicorn saw this and groaned.

The end.

About the Author

I am a retired barrister. I love football. I am married to my wife. I have a stepson, a son and a daughter. I originally come from Bebington, Wirral but I have now lived and worked in Cambridgeshire for almost 30 years. In my youth, I used to write a little and I would wonder about writing a humorous book. Work and life events meant this never happened until now. Retirement from the law has given me the time and inspirational space to fulfil my dream. I've had fun writing it and I hope you have fun reading it too!